'You're a
desirable won

'No male with a millilitre of red blood in his
wouldn't burn at the sight of you!' Simon said.

He reached out for Anna, seizing her roughly,
bringing his mouth to hers in a kiss that was
devoid of tenderness—a kiss that was angry and
thrusting, hurting her with its force. And
yet. . .and yet she responded to it just as forcefully—matching anger with anger, passion with
passion.

When his heat was no longer slammed against her
own, she reacted by saying, 'I don't want to be out
of control like that—I don't want sex for kicks,
without love. . .and I don't want it with you!'

Janet Ferguson was born at Newmarket, Suffolk. She nursed as a VAD during the Second World War, then became a medical secretary, working in hospitals in London and the provinces, but is now retired and lives near Brighton. She has had a number of novels published, but she finds medical romances the most satisfying and interesting to plot.

Recent titles by the same author:

LABOUR OF LOVE
DOCTOR AT SEFTONBRIDGE

A SURGEON TO TRUST

BY
JANET FERGUSON

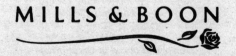

DID YOU PURCHASE THIS BOOK WITHOUT A COVER?
If you did, you should be aware it is **stolen property** as it was
reported *unsold and destroyed* by a retailer. Neither the Author
nor the publisher has received any payment for this book.

All the characters in this book have no existence outside the imagination of the author, and have no relation whatsoever to anyone bearing the same name or names. They are not even distantly inspired by any individual known or unknown to the author, and all the incidents are pure invention.

All Rights Reserved including the right of reproduction in whole or in part in any form. This edition is published by arrangement with Harlequin Enterprises II B.V. The text of this publication or any part thereof may not be reproduced or transmitted in any form or by any means, electronic or mechanical, including photocopying, recording, storage in an information retrieval system, or otherwise, without the written permission of the publisher.

This book is sold subject to the condition that it shall not, by way of trade or otherwise, be lent, resold, hired out or otherwise circulated without the prior consent of the publisher in any form of binding or cover other than that in which it is published and without a similar condition including this condition being imposed on the subsequent purchaser.

MILLS & BOON and MILLS & BOON with the Rose Device are registered trademarks of the publisher.

First published in Great Britain 1996
Harlequin Mills & Boon Limited,
Eton House, 18-24 Paradise Road, Richmond, Surrey TW9 1SR

© Janet Ferguson 1996

ISBN 0 263 80015 6

Set in Times 10 on 11 pt. by
Rowland Phototypesetting Limited
Bury St Edmunds, Suffolk

03-9702-50740-D

Printed and bound in Great Britain
by Mackays of Chatham PLC, Chatham

CHAPTER ONE

IT WAS the end of June when Anna Fellowes took up the post of Sister on the gynae ward of the Regent Hospital, Charding. Her husband had died two years previously, and she supposed she could say she was getting over it. . .whatever that might mean.

It was sensible, she felt, to have made this move to the south coast. Charding was an important town, with plenty of interests. She had her own self-contained flat, too, in Prue Gatton's—her grandmother's—house, which was less than a mile from the hospital, no distance with a car.

The hospital, eight-hundred-bedded and serving a wide area, had the sea at its front, the Downs at its rear and a view of the town at one end. Some people said that on a clear day the Normandy coast could be glimpsed from the top of the tower block, but Anna had yet to prove this to be true.

Even more importantly she had yet to prove herself, for this was her first Ward Sister's post and only her second day. She was, however, being helped and advised by the retiring sister, Ruth Hilton, who had just gone off to lunch. After today she would be on her own, which was slightly alarming. Still, she'd been nursing at the Walbrook in London in a senior staffing position, *and* on a gynae ward, so she didn't feel out of place, nor too daunted, and it was vital to progress.

Even so, a ward of strange patients, when met up with all at once, took some getting used to, and it was necessary to study all the case-notes and set a face to each one. This was what she was doing as she sat in the office during the start of the quiet hour, just before visiting time.

The nursing staff had all welcomed her warmly when she'd met them yesterday. The registrar and house officer had been affable as well, but she had yet to meet the consultant, Simon Easter, who was away on a long weekend.

'He's a natural charmer,' Jean Ross, the staff nurse, had told her. 'He's the knight-in-shining-armour type— the kind of man you dream about and think "if only" in the middle of the night. He's unattached too. . .well, divorced, anyway. . .' she rolled her eyes heavenwards '. . .and, added to all this, he's a brilliant surgeon. I once saw him deliver triplets, and I've never forgotten it.'

Anna rated the last-named considerably higher than Jean's droolings about shining knights. Charming men were usually vain as well, and far too sure of themselves. They also tended to be unfaithful and weak in certain respects.

Daniel, for instance, had been charming-plus, but he'd broken his marriage vows, and every promise he'd ever made, and Anna's heart as well. And yet. . .and yet. . . And she sighed as her thoughts strayed back to him and she pictured his face and form as though he were standing in front of her eyes. . . And yet she had stayed in love with him till he died.

She was over him now, though; she was free now, free to do her job, and perhaps—for stranger things often happened—perhaps one day she would get married again—to a quieter man, whom she could turn to and trust.

Never look back, Prue Gatton, her grandmother, had advised, and how right she was. . . I've done with all that. . . Anna swivelled her chair away from the desk to face the window, which looked out on to the ward. It was an old-type Nightingale ward, consisting of two long lines of beds and a wide aisle down the middle.

At the ward desk, or nurses' station, Lee Cheng— the little Thai nurse—was busy filing reports. Jean was unwrapping a beribboned bouquet which had come for Mrs Dodds in bed five who, too weak to care, opened her eyes and smiled. The beds had been tidied; most patients were dozing, or reading, or watching the doors.

Janice Hall, the second-year nurse—head held high— was taking a covered bedpan out to the sluice. Janice was thinking of giving up nursing, and Anna had made a note to talk to her about this as soon as possible. Quite a few learners were tempted to give up after their first year.

Anna herself had nearly done so, but how thankful she was that she'd resisted and carried on and made the grade at last. Now, at twenty-seven years old, she had her own ward. She was still amazed that she'd been chosen from so many applicants.

She glanced down at her dress of thick purple cotton and put a careful hand to her cap, which—tiny and frilled—sat on the top of her head like a puff of cloud. Her jaw-length bob, which had a slight wave, was the colour of new pennies, whilst her eyes—hazel-brown and lavishly lashed—were the widespaced, thoughtful kind. She was tall and slender, with beautiful legs.

'You walk like an angel, dear,' old Mrs Fotheringay had told her yesterday. Alice Fotheringay was in one of the side-wards, and as the door was always open she had a good view of everyone passing up and down the corridor.

'No wings to take the weight off my feet, though,' Anna had said with a grimace, finding time to talk to the little woman who in ten days' time was being transferred to a hospice on the other side of town.

Alice was a sad case and thinking about her now, Anna got up to take her notes out of the filing cabinet. She was just pushing the drawer in, with her back towards the door, when she heard someone enter and, turning round and expecting to see Ruth Hilton, she found herself looking at a tall blond man, who at first flying glimpse reminded her of Daniel—could have *been* Daniel—and the shock of it made her gasp. It paled her face too; made her hands shake; made her drop the file over her feet.

He came round the desk to her, looking surprised. 'I seem to have startled you.'

'Most people knock,' she said pointedly, feeling the kind of irrational anger which sometimes follows shock.

He said nothing, but squatted down and helped her pick up the file. Meeting his eyes at haunch level, she glimpsed in their slatey depths a gleam of curiosity which was mirrored in her own.

He was smartly dressed and had a spruce, brushed look. He was a visitor, no doubt, an early visitor who perhaps wanted to speak to someone in charge. And that someone was her, Sister Fellowes. Pulling herself together, she was about to ask him what he wanted when Ruth came into the room with a cry of, 'Why Mr *Easter*, did you have a good weekend?'

'I did.' He was still looking enquiringly at Anna and, taking this to mean that he'd only just come and that they'd not been introduced, Ruth leapt into the breach.

'This is Mrs Anna Fellowes, Mr Easter—she takes over from me tomorrow. Sister, this is Mr Easter, our consultant.' She ranged herself at his side.

'Welcome to the Regent, Sister Fellowes.' His hand came over the desk and now the look in his eyes was clear amusement, whilst his face—the bendable kind—softened into creases as he smiled.

Taking his hand in a kind of trance, Anna wondered how she could possibly have thought he was anything *like* Daniel. This man had laughter lines radiating out from his eyes, a wide, even-lipped mouth, and a tiny scar to the right of his chin. His hair was fawn, not fair. . . dun-coloured hair, like an animal's pelt, lying close and flat to his head.

As she thanked him for his welcome she remembered how she'd spoken to him earlier on—how she'd virtually told him off for not knocking before entering the office— and she felt her whole body go hot. Her discomfiture was noticed by a watching Ruth, who tactlessly enquired if she was all right and, before Anna could nod, went on to say, 'Not feeling the strain already, I hope,' thereby hinting that there was worse to come and that her young successor wouldn't be up to it.

'It's a little hot in here, don't you think?' Anna said quietly and decided to ignore Ruth's little dig, even when she said,

'Well, the windows open easily enough,' and pushed at the metal arm, then turned round to Simon Easter with a shrug and a long-suffering smile. 'I expect you've come to see Mrs Miller, sir?' She found the notes on the desk, then glanced at Anna. 'You stay where you are, and tackle this paperwork. *I'll* chaperon Mr Easter— the last thing we want is to have you keeling over in the ward.'

'That's unlikely to happen.' Anna walked round the desk. She was taller than Ruth, which gave her an advantage and a certain imperiousness. 'I'd like to start as I mean to go on, Ruth. I'll escort Mr Easter. I'm sure you can do with a rest; you've been trailing around after me all day.' This was said with a smile but her eyes were challenging and she held out her hand for the notes, which an astonished Ruth passed over to her, even managing to mutter her thanks.

'I doubt if Ruth has been overridden like that for many a year,' Simon commented drily, out in the corridor.

'She meant well; she's been very helpful to me,' was all Anna said, affording him a view of her long, narrow back as she preceded him into the ward.

Karen Miller was thirty-seven years old and seventeen weeks into her first pregnancy, and Anna had seen from her notes that she and her husband had been trying for a baby for over ten years. During her first trimester, however, an ovarian tumour had been diagnosed at a routine check in the antenatal clinic. She had been referred to Simon who, because of the risk of precipitating a miscarriage during her first three months, had decided to delay surgery until now.

This afternoon he wanted to talk to her and reassure her as much as he could. Her appearance certainly reassured *him* for she looked the picture of health—younger than her age, with rosy cheeks and boyishly cut curly hair. After the usual greetings she plied him with questions. 'It is a *benign* tumour, isn't it, Doctor. . .? There's no question of malignancy?'

'I expect to find a benign cyst.' He was choosing his words carefully, Anna noticed, as he sat on the edge of the bed.

He was different on the ward, she also noticed, but, then, most doctors were. Some of them postured but Simon Easter didn't—he was approachable and kind, yet detached enough, impersonal enough, to stop at source any natural female embarrassment which his patient might feel.

'And you'll be able to get it away without harming the baby?' Anxiety clouded Karen Miller's dark eyes, which looked towards Anna as well. 'I want it so much—

we both do; we've been trying for so long. I was thrilled
when I found I'd taken at last, and then this. . .this *thing*
had to come.'

'You're in good hands,' Anna averred, saving Simon
from having to dissemble again, and she caught his
approving glance.

'Now, that,' he said, smiling as he got up from the
bed, 'is what I was bursting to say but modesty prevailed!
This time tomorrow—' he looked down at Karen '—it'll
be all over and you'll wonder what you worried about.
Try and get some rest, or get on with this.' He handed
over to her the beginnings of a shawl on big knitting
pins, which she'd been working on when he appeared.

'It's almost certainly a corpus luteum,' he told Anna
at the ward desk. 'There's a risk to the foetus in removing
it, but merely to sit on the fence and leave it *in situ*
would be to risk torsion when she goes into labour. By
now, with luck, the placenta should be secreting enough
hormone to keep the pregnancy going without help from
the ovary. Even so, with a couple who've found it hard
to conceive and who want a child so much, it's a dam-
nable thing to have happened when they should be
feeling on top of the world.'

'I agree; it is.' She took the notes from him, thinking
as she did so and glimpsing his concerned face, that he
wasn't an unfeeling man. He plainly thought of his
patients as human, not merely as chunks of interesting
material on which to demonstrate his skills.

'Have you come across a case like this before?' he
asked as they walked to the doors.

She nodded. 'Yes, we had a case at the Walbrook,
where I was nursing before. The patient was a girl of
twenty, only ten weeks into her pregnancy, but it was
necessary to operate at once due to pain from twisting.
Everyone thought she'd miscarry, but the foetus was

undisturbed. Progestogens were given with complete success, and she went on to full term.'

'Was the surgery performed by Sir Michael Doveton, by any chance?' Simon's voice came close to her ear as he leaned to open the door.

'Yes, it was.' She brushed past him into the corridor.

'I know him,' he said. 'He's a brilliant surgeon, and the Walbrook's a cracking hospital.'

'Mmm,' she nodded, 'I was sorry to leave it.'

'So why did you?' he asked. He was poised to go— was half turned away—but waited for her answer. 'Perhaps,' he prompted, 'your husband got moved to Charding and it was a case of Hobson's choice?'

'It was my choice,' Anna told him, backing into the office. 'I wanted a ward manager's post *and* to live in Sussex. My husband died two years ago, so I'd only myself to please.'

'Oh, I see; I didn't realise.' His eyes were on her wedding ring, visible on the hand that held the green folder of notes. 'It's not always the happiest of situations when we have only ourselves to please,' he said, reinforcing what Anna had realised over the past two years.

'It's like having too much rope,' she admitted. 'There are times when you don't know what to do with all of it—at least, not for the best.'

'Well, let's hope that life at the Regent will take up some of the slack,' he said, looking up towards the end of the corridor where one of the lifts was disgorging its first load of visitors, filling the landing outside. 'I'm off before I get caught up in that lot!' He smiled at her and was off, striding up the corridor straight and tall and with such an air of purpose that he all but cut a swathe through the incoming crowd.

He's the kind of man for whom everyone stands aside, Anna thought, leaving the door of the office ajar in case any of the visitors wanted to see her, and within minutes one of them did. He was a Mr Alex Marriner and he had come, Anna knew, to see his housekeeper, Miss Rayland, who had undergone surgery for stress incontinence.

In fact, Anna had already met Alex last week when she had first arrived in Charding. She had gone to his very prestigious shop—Marriners' Antiques, owned by him and his father—to buy a gift for Prue. Alex had taken pains to advise her, as had his father, the result being that she had gone home with a small porcelain jug which both father and son—who knew her grand-mother—assured her she would love.

He looked, Anna noticed, a shade ill at ease this after-noon, but then lone men often did when up on the gynae floor. She thought it was good of him to visit, especially as Miss Rayland would most likely be discharged next day and under his roof once more.

'We shan't allow her to do a thing, of course,' he said, when Anna had explained—without giving any medical details—how his housekeeper was. 'We've got a "daily" coming in for a time, and neither my father nor I, nor young Tom for that matter, are helpless domestically.'

'I know she's looking forward to being with you again,' Anna told him with truth, for Imogen Rayland hadn't taken kindly to hospital routine.

A frown drew vertical lines on Alex Marriner's brow. He had a high forehead, accentuated by the brushed-back style of his hair. He was a widower—Prue had told Anna this—and had lost his wife in an accident when his son, Tom, was only five years old. He and Tom—now nearly nine—and his father, Charles Marriner, lived in a ram-bling old stone-built house a few miles out of town.

Anna watched him saunter into the ward, squaring

himself to the task but quickening his pace when, from
bed number twelve, Miss Rayland raised her hand. He
was an attractive man in a mature, laid-back kind of
way. Nothing much would ruffle him. Anna could
imagine him bidding coolly at auction sales, and never
getting fazed.

It's surprising he's not married again, passed through
her mind just as Ruth came in with a box of chocolates,
which she dumped down on the desk. 'I'm still collecting
goodbye gifts,' she said, making out that she couldn't
care less, but it was obvious that she was pleased.

'Good for you,' Anna said warmly, their little clash
of wills not forgotten but brushed out of sight as they
exchanged wary smiles. Anna knew that Ruth had had
her formal presentation party; she also knew that the
nurses had organised another, less formal, affair for later
on this afternoon up here on the ward.

She, Anna, wasn't staying for it; she felt it was tactful
to make herself scarce on such an occasion so, as soon
as her shift ended at a little after four-thirty, she wished
Ruth well and left.

Outside in the slanting sunshine that paled her hair to
gilt, she got right to the car park before she remembered
that she'd travelled in by bus that morning, having lent
her car to Prue. 'Oh, damn!' she swore out loud. It was
all very well getting the bus at the start of the day when
you were bright-eyed and bushy-tailed, but quite another
to queue for it in the evening when you were tired and
fit to drop.

Still, it wouldn't kill her, she supposed, and she began
to cut diagonally across the tarmac to reach the exit
gates. She was looking at the gates and not at the cars,
and as she reached the doctors' bay she was all but
knocked flying by a cream BMW, backing out of the
parking line.

'Do you usually stroll about on a car park as though it's a country lane?' was barked at her from the rolled-down window, and for the second time that day Consultant Simon Easter and the new Sister Fellowes stared at one another in a state of semi-shock.

'No, of course not.' Anna found her voice. 'I came for my car and found it wasn't here.' She picked up her bag, which had slithered off her shoulder, and backed out of his way.

'Do you mean it's been taken...stolen?' He swung his legs out of the car and stood in front of her, looming a little and blocking out the sun.

'No, nothing like that,' she said quickly. 'I just forgot I'd not brought it today. I lent it to my grandmother this morning—hers has gone in for its MOT.'

'I see.' He pursed his mouth thoughtfully, as though in sympathy, but his tone seemed to indicate that he thought her an absent-minded twit, which wasn't, she sighed, very far from the truth but she'd had a harassing day. Still shading her eyes and wishing she could shade the rest of herself off from him, she backed away, apologising for giving him such a shock.

'Evens the score!' His eyes took her in as she stood there in the sun, softly rounded, tall and slim in her purple uniform dress. He remembered the look on her face when he'd startled her in the office. It had been a panicky look, almost of fright, as though she were seeing a ghost. Yet she wasn't, he felt, the panicky sort and, with a wish to make amends and feeling curious about her too, he asked her where she lived.

'Romsey Road. There's a bus that leaves the Aquarium at five. I'd better make tracks.'

She half turned, then heard him say, 'Look, I'll run you home. I live in Andover Square, so it's on my way... Save you waiting around.' He leaned into his car, unlocked the passenger door then came round and opened it wide. 'In you get,' he said cheerfully, his hand on the catch.

The car's elegant cream interior filled Anna's vision. She didn't want a lift, not with him. She didn't want the chore of having to make conversation all the way to Romsey Road. There was something else too, like a sliver of warning, that kept her rooted to the tarmac— she didn't want to get to know him one fraction more than she did at this moment. She didn't want the slightest off-the-ward involvement. It was best to play safe.

'I'm relatively harmless, Sister Fellowes. . . Are you coming with me, or not? Perhaps you have a passion for riding on buses!' And now he was laughing at her and small wonder, for she must look ridiculous standing there all of a droop.

'A lift would be brilliant; it was just that I felt I shouldn't bother you,' she told him with a mixture of firmness and sweetness as she dipped her head under that glittering, baking-hot roof and sank down into opulence.

'So, you've a grandmother here in Charding,' he said as he eased the car through the exit gates and out onto a side street which led down to the main coast road.

'Yes, I have. I live with her,' Anna explained. 'With her and yet separately, which is the best way of all. She has one of those tall Victorian houses in Romsey Road. She lives on the ground floor and the other two floors are let off as flats. I've got the one at the top—it's completely self-contained. Having a flat to move into made all the difference in the world.'

'I expect Mrs. . . I expect your grandmother is glad of your company,' he said with his eye on the coach in front of them, which was hogging most of the road. It was the time of evening when families were coming off the beach and piers, whilst the busy road which ran eastwards to the port and beyond was awash with rush-hour traffic and the inevitable coaches.

'She's Mrs Gatton, my paternal grandmother.' They were passing the coach, rushing along by its blue and red side, then pulling in beyond it behind a car with a dinghy lashed to its roof. 'Prue, that's what I call her—' Anna felt it was safe to go on '—isn't really the sort to need my company; she's got loads of friends of her own. Her mother, my great-grandmother, lives in a home out at Morley Down. That's why Prue needed a car today—to go and visit her. She goes every Tuesday. Great-Nan is ninety-nine.'

'A great age. . . Can she still get around?'

'On a Zimmer, yes, she can.'

'Of course people are living longer these days,' Simon remarked, not bothering with the usual off-the-cuff comment about how wonderful it was. Great-Nan didn't think it was wonderful and neither—if she was honest—did Prue who, up until a year ago, had looked after her mother herself.

'So, there are three generations of us,' Anna said, filling in the silence that fell between them as Simon braked at the lights.

'Not four, then?' He turned his head and she felt his eyes on her face.

'I haven't a child, if that's what you mean,' she said flatly, staring ahead. 'I was pregnant when my husband was killed, but the shock made me abort.'

'A wretched time for you.' His eyes left her face as the lights flicked from amber to red. He eased the car forward, then asked her, 'Was it a road accident?'

'No, a hotel fire. Daniel was in France on business. He was an international accountant, so was often away from home.' Her explanation was still a flat statement, for in no way did she want any more sympathetic noises—or questions, come to that.

Perhaps recognising this, Simon Easter, who was by
no means insensitive, merely said, 'What a terrible thing
to happen,' and left it at that.

Once past the Palace Pier the traffic thinned a little,
and he was able to make the turn into Romsey Road
without too much hassle. It was a tree-lined road, with
houses of the Victorian Gothic type rising up from behind
tall hedges which shaded long front lawns. Over Prue
Gatton's porch hung a swathe of clematis, pale mauve
and delicately foliaged. 'Now take a look at *that*!' Simon
exclaimed, about to cruise by—not realising, until Anna
stopped him, that this was her grandmother's house.

'Here she is now; here's Prue,' Anna said as she spotted her yellow sports car tearing up the road.

Prue Gatton had the hood back and as she turned in
at the kerb they could see her sitting behind the wheel,
thin brown arms emerging from a print cotton dress and
a bandeau confining her hair. Her smile flashed white
in her tanned face when she saw her granddaughter. Then
with both cars stationary, they all got out and Anna made
the necessary introductions, watching Simon and Prue
shake hands.

'I'm afraid I stole Anna's car today.' Prue's glance at
Simon appeared to be the quick and polite kind, but it
missed very little. She liked his eyes, which narrowed
into crinkles when he smiled. She approved, too, of his
handshake and of his deep-toned masculine voice.

'I seized my chance, and gave her a lift.' His smile
included them both. 'I live in Andover Square, though,
so it was virtually on my way home.'

'It's all doctors, and dentists and physios there. It
should be called Harley Square,' Prue said, and he
laughed out loud but agreed with her as well. 'My house,
which I took over from my predecessor,' he said, 'is

very similar to yours but I can't, alas—' he glanced up
the path '—boast a clematis over my porch.'

'It *is* rather lovely, isn't it?' Prue said, well pleased.
'Of course, the trick with clematis is to clip it hard back
in the autumn, you know. Are you a gardener as well as
a surgeon, Mr Easter? How do you find the time?'

'With difficulty,' he said, looking at Anna, who
couldn't hide her surprise.

'Surely you have to guard your hands. . .? I mean,
bearing in mind. . .' Her voice tailed off as she saw
him nod.

'I'm very careful indeed, but then all gardeners should
be. Wearing protective gloves should be a must for
anyone working with garden soil.'

'Hear, hear!' Prue applauded, and Anna nearly choked
for her grandmother took no precautions at all when
engrossed in her gardening chores. The protective gloves,
which she'd bought her last summer when she'd been
down on holiday, were nearly always left on the bench
in the potting shed. The trouble with the over-seventies
is that they just won't be advised, she was thinking as
she heard Prue asking Simon if he'd like to come through
to the back.

'I've a purple clematis trained round an arbour that
I'm rather proud of,' she said.

He'll say 'no' for certain, Anna thought. He'll thank
her and take his leave. He won't want to hang about at
this time of evening, looking at climbing plants.

But it seemed that he did and, more than that, he was
keen. 'I'd love to see it,' he said, so up the garden
path they trooped, into the house and through the cool
cavernous hall to the glass doors at the end. Prue
unlocked the doors, pushing them outwards—she did
everything with force—and then they were out in the
sun again, going down shallow steps into the walled

garden where the clematis, so darkly purple that it was very nearly black, rioted over the arbour which Prue had knocked together herself.

'My word, yes, it's a beauty!' Simon exclaimed, then showed so much interest in the garden generally that Prue took him on a tour. Anna walked along slightly behind them, allowing Prue full rein, amazed at the way her grandmother—who could be offhand and dour at times—appeared to have come under Simon Easter's spell. She was all set for taking him into the orchard when from back inside the house came the chirruping sound of the telephone bell. 'Oh, drat the thing!' She swung round.

'I'll answer it,' Anna offered.

Prue shook her head, 'No, I'd better; it'll be Marriners' Antiques. They were bidding for something for me today and they said they'd ring.' She was calling this over her shoulder as she ran flat-footedly over the lawn, leaving Anna and Simon at the entrance to the orchard where the grass grew thick and long.

'It's like a jungle in there; I think we'd better give it a miss,' Anna said, fearing for Simon's suit. 'You need jeans in there, as well as high boots and a scythe to hack your way through!'

'A slight exaggeration, but I get your drift,' he laughed, his shadow merging with hers as they turned and looked back at the house.

The garden was full of summer sounds—the hiss of a water sprinkler, the snip of shears from over the wall, the hum of a power mower. They could see Prue in the dimness of the hall, talking on the phone. Directly overhead, from the open windows of the first-floor flat, came the strains of the six o'clock news. 'My flat's at the top,' Anna said, well aware that she was repeating herself, but in Prue's absence she had to keep talking hard.

'You'll get a fine view.' He looked up at the two sash windows, each one set under the slope of a gable, which gave the house its name.

'Oh, I do—the best.' She seized on that. 'I can see the sea between the piers. I've got two sitting-rooms, a bedroom and a bathroom, plus a modern kitchen. The previous tenant was an artist—he used the north sitting-room as a studio.'

'Interesting!' Simon switched his gaze from the upper reaches of the house to Anna. 'Which came first,' he asked her, 'the job or the flat?'

'Well, actually, the flat,' she admitted. 'Prue had told me it was empty. She knew I wanted to move out of London and then that very same week I saw the sister/charge nurse post advertised in the *Nursing Times*.'

'Sometimes, just sometimes,' he said, 'life dishes out what we want—not exactly on a plate, perhaps, but it's there for the taking—providing we have the courage to grab it.'

'Yes, that's very true.'

'And you did, so well done!'

'Thank you.' He was saying all the right things and she wondered why he was bothering, but maybe she shouldn't be quite so suspicious of praise when it came from a male. 'Have you been in Charding long?' she asked, genuinely wanting to know.

'Three years.' He brushed a leaf from his sleeve and watched it flutter down. 'I took over the house from my predecessor, together with his private patients. My quarters are on the ground floor, the consulting-rooms over the top and over those are the attics, unused at the moment. I've far too much space, of course, although part of it's filled, during the day, by my secretary/nurse and by my housekeeper, Mrs Gill. It's a whole world away from my Kensington flat,' he added with a smile.

'Oh, you were in London. . . Which hospital?' Anna heard herself ask.

'I was a senior registrar at Queens',' he informed her, 'but like you I wanted a change. I'd also set my heart on a consultancy.'

'Which you got.'

'By the skin of my teeth.'

'Skin, or not, you got it,' she said, making him laugh.

'You make a good champion, Anna.'

'Which you're not, I think, in any need of,' she told him, smiling, just as her grandmother, having finished on the telephone, came hurrying back over the grass.

'It was Claytons Garage,' she said, 'going on and on about all they've had to do to the Renault to make it fit for the road. It's a load of nonsense, I'm quite sure; they're just giving themselves a job. Anyway, it's done and ready to pick up.' She looked hopefully at Anna, just as Simon glanced at his watch and said that it was time he was off.

'I've a patient due at seven,' he said, shaking hands with Prue again. 'Your garden is a credit to you, Mrs Gatton. Thank you for letting me see it.'

'You can have some cuttings off the clematis in the autumn,' she told him at the gate, watching him angle his long legs into his shiny cream car. He thanked her, said goodbye to them both and then drew away from the kerb, making for Andover Square and home via the top of the road.

'Nice man—beautiful manners,' Prue said a few minutes later when Anna was driving her to Severndean to pick up the car.

'His beautiful manners, alias his charm, are part of his stock-in-trade,' Anna said. The on-shore wind cooled her cheeks and she gratefully drew it in.

'Is he married?' Prue persisted.

'Divorced, so I'm told.'

'There's a lot of it about,' Prue asserted, as though it was some kind of flu. 'Looking as he does, I dare say he'd get plenty of chances to stray. Even so, he doesn't strike me as being the sort to cheat on a woman.'

'You can't possibly tell that on such short acquaintance.' Anna pulled in to let an ambulance pass in a blare of sound and, glancing at her face, Prue remembered Daniel Fellowes and changed the subject fast.

CHAPTER TWO

COPING without Ruth Hilton's hovering presence next day was far more challenging and scary than Anna had thought. From the moment of taking the hand-over report from Night Sister Poole everything rested on her; became *her* responsibility.

It was she, Anna, who had to set the nurses on their various tasks. It was to her they turned for advice... 'Sister, Mrs Tooley won't let me shave her'...'Sister, there are ketones in Mrs Park's urine'...'Sister, we're low on sheets'.

The telephone never stopped ringing; one of the pharmacists—a disagreeable, know-all type—came to query a prescription. Added to this, it was the main operating day, which meant that Miss Tell, the SNO, came to do her round early—sweeping in and out of the ward flinging 'good mornings' right and left, asking Anna about the bed-list, and would she get hers up to date?

No sooner had she gone than Meg Brodie, the house officer, made her appearance. Jet-haired, Scottish and plump, with a white coat that didn't meet in front, she commiserated with Anna about the hassle of being new.

'Still, doon't you worry, Sister,' she smiled, showing healthy teeth. 'You'll not be bothered with the surgeons today; they've got a theatre list as long as your arm and back again, as of course you'll be knowing.'

'Yes, I know,' Anna said ruefully, watching Karen Miller being lifted on to a theatre trolley and wheeled away to the doors.

'She's nairvous, is that one.' Meg, with hay fever, sneezed very loudly, then blew her nose like a horn.

'She's nervous of the outcome, not of the actual op. Mr Easter. . .' Anna's voice altered slightly '. . .spent time with her yesterday, explaining what he was going to do and generally cheering her up.'

'He's a naice man—great to work for, explains things all the taime, and he's no too big for his theatre boots like some consultants are. Even Bill likes him.' Bill Corby, Anna knew, was Simon's registrar. 'And that's amazing,' Meg continued, 'for when the consultancy came up Bill hoped to get it—was *expected* to get it— but Simon pipped him at the post. Bill does most of the obstetric work, which is usually run-of-the-mill.'

'It's a rat race, like any other. . .getting on in the medical world,' Anna said, thinking that, quite aside from his considerable experience, Simon would sell himself well to a selecting panel, and she couldn't help feeling a certain sympathy for the more timid Bill Corby, still having to be number two.

The morning progressed. Karen came back from Theatre; Mrs Jacobs, in for a fibroidectomy, went down. Mrs Tooley, due for a total hysterectomy, had submitted at last to being shaved and would be next on the list. Lying there in her theatre gown, a white cap confining her hair, she looked fretful and unhappy with her pale eyes full of fear. 'My 'usband'll go right orf me, dear—' she caught at Anna's hand '—wot with no hair down below, and now 'arf of me about to be chucked in the rubbish bin, he won't fancy me no more.'

'Mrs Tooley—' Anna sat on the edge of her bed '—your pubic hair will grow again at the rate of knots, and as for half of you being chucked in the bin, that's not the case at all. What *is* being taken away won't show and won't affect the way your husband feels about you, nor the way you feel about him.'

'It won't be the same.'

'You may find it'll be a whole lot better,' Anna con-
soled, with her eye on Jean Ross, who'd arrived with
the pre-med tray. 'It's all right, Jean, I'll see to this.'
She took the syringe from the dish then, rolling Mrs
Tooley onto her side, she injected the powerful drug into
her buttock, giving it a quick rub.

'Do what they like with you 'ere, they do,' Mrs Tooley
grumbled. 'Nothing's sacred for two minutes; even your
backside's not yer own!'

Cautioning her not to try to get out of bed, Anna drew
her curtains and left her to drift into haziness till the
porters came for her.

Shortly before the big luncheon trolley was trundled into
the ward Alex Marriner arrived to fetch Miss Rayland,
who had been ready since ten a.m. Anna wheeled her
out to the lift, which wasn't strictly necessary but the
poor woman still had stitches *in situ*, which made walking hell. 'I can't wait to get back to normal living,' she
said, as though she had been in hospital half a year
instead of only three days.

Goodbyes and thanks were said at the lifts. 'I'll be in
touch,' Alex called out to Anna just before the doors
slid to. She wondered why and what he had meant, then
he slipped from her mind as Miss Tell, who'd arrived
by the stairs, asked her if she could make her remaining
side-ward ready for a patient from Maternity.

'She gave birth to a stillborn child an hour ago,' she
explained. 'Sister Webb is anxious for her not to have
to stay in the postnatal ward, within sight and sound of
the well babies, and I must say I agree.'

'Yes, of course. Oh, poor woman!' Anna said, then
found that she was talking to Miss Tell's back, for

already she had turned and was making for the stairhead again.

Nurse Cheng and Nurse Hall got the second of the side-wards aired and ready and a call from Maternity confirmed that Mrs Johnson would be coming down after lunch. Mrs Tooley was wheeled to the theatre suite, Mrs Jacobs came up and Mrs Fotheringay developed breathing difficulties and was given oxygen. Her heart rate was slow and Anna sent for Meg, who wasn't happy about her. 'She needs specialling, but we haven't the staff. She should be in a hospice *now*,' she said, frowning, and hung her charts back on the end of the bed.

At last—at long last—it was time for Anna's own lunch. Resisting the temptation to skip it, as she had the day before, she made her way up to the fifth floor and the staff cafeteria. The immense dining-room, like a long hall, was divided into bays by partitions and fancy trellis-work, like the top of a garden fence.

Finding her way into the sisters' section, laden with her tray, Anna sat down with Rose Webb from Maternity and Carla Scott from the children's ward. Rose apologised for offloading one of her patients into Anna's ward.

'I've got a side ward free, so no problem,' Anna said, cutting into her portion of toad-in-the-hole and wishing she'd chosen salad instead.

'Her husband's with her—refuses to leave her—so you'll be lumbered with him as well. They're only eighteen and nineteen—just a pair of kids.'

'Plenty of time, then,' Carla Scott broke in, 'for them to have healthy kids later on.'

'That isn't the whole of the story, though, is it?' Anna started to say, but didn't finish for Rose was asking her how she was getting on, and had she met Simon Easter yet, and wasn't she the lucky one to have him in her ward most days?

Carefully Anna agreed that she was, and equally carefully said that she had met him yesterday but forbore to mention that he'd run her home and been shown the back windows of her flat.

'He's not married, you know...at least, not now,' Rose mumbled through a mouthful of lettuce. 'He hasn't got any kids, either, so no encumbrances.'

'I see.' Anna took note.

'It's mostly work with him; he's the dedicated type, although he has a flip side—knows how to enjoy himself. He's been seen around with some pretty slick girls—the Sloaney, designer-clothes sort, long-legged and glossy— but never *one* in particular. Looking like he does, being who he is, he can probably take his pick. He never dates anyone from the hospital, though, so I guess he likes to keep work and play in separate spheres.'

'Considering the gossip, I don't blame him,' Anna said with an edge to her voice, not missed by Carla Scott who—looking slyly through her bifocals—made the remark:

'Of course he may relax his rule with Anna, looking as she does. Gynae hasn't had a sister under menopause age for many a long year!'

'I heed the compliment,' Anna laughed, but was relieved when Rose began to talk about Ellen Johnson who'd had the stillborn child.

'She was told in Clinic yesterday that the foetus was dead. The midwife couldn't get a heartbeat, and a scan confirmed the worst. She was brought in late last night, and was about to be induced when she went into spontaneous labour and gave birth two hours ago.'

'What time will she be coming down to me?' Anna asked.

'I thought, if it's all right with you, soon after we get back. She might have visitors this afternoon in the shape of her parents but at the moment, as I told you, her husband is being hyper-protective.'

'So he should be at such a ghastly time,' Anna said, and Rose agreed.

Soon after lunch, during the quiet hour, Ellen Johnson was wheeled into number two side-ward by her young husband and helped into bed. She had been washed and tidied in Maternity but still had the look of having been through the wringer, whilst her husband, Hal, was almost as ravaged as she was and equally prone to tears.

Theirs was a case, Anna decided, when sympathy conveyed by touch and a welcoming voice was less upsetting than a spate of words, which might come out all wrong. If Ellen wished to talk about it she could, but just now she plainly did not.

'You'll be quiet in here—private, too.' Anna switched on a cooling fan for the afternoon was hot and humid; it was difficult to breathe. 'If you want anything press your bell, and someone will be with you at once.'

They thanked her and she went out, quietly closing the door —which was against the rules but Ellen wasn't ill; all she needed was rest and quiet.

Simon came on the ward at four-thirty, mainly to see Karen Miller. Although changed out of his theatre clothes, it seemed to Anna that he bore traces of having hurried to do so—his hair was tousled in front, his tie didn't lie absolutely straight and he smelled of Hibiscrub. 'I hoped to catch you before you went off duty,' he said. 'I'd like to see Mrs Miller, and also Alice Fotheringay. Meg told me about Alice's breathing difficulties; I'm not happy about her at all.'

'She seems easier now and doesn't need her oxygen; she's being checked quarter-hourly,' Anna told him, getting out the two sets of notes.

'OK, then.' Simon took them from her. 'Karen Miller

first. 'That tumour of hers was benign, a corpus luteum as we thought. Her baby's safely tucked up inside her, and I see no reason why she shouldn't go on to full term with no problems at all.'

'Yes, I saw that from the theatre notes. . .' Anna started to say, but Simon was already walking into the ward and she hurried to catch him up.

Karen, still sleepy, was able to take his words in but only managed one of her own. 'Magic!' she said, smiling faintly, dark eyes shining between half-closed lids.

Simon glanced briefly at the charts of five of the other post-op patients, after which he and Anna proceeded to the side-wards—running into Nurse Cheng who was leaving Alice Fotheringay's bed. 'She is awake and had asked for a drink,' she said, and went across the corridor to get it.

What happened next was to stay imprinted on Anna's mind for days. As she entered the side-ward, Simon behind her, Alice Fotheringay raised herself from her mound of pillows, smiled and then fell back—eyes fixed, pallid-faced—as though struck by an unseen hand.

'*Arrested.* . . Ring team!' Simon's hand was at the pulse spot on Alice's neck. Nurse Cheng returned and flew to the phone, whilst Anna jerked the pillows from under Alice's head then watched Simon begin the thumping movements of sternal massage, using the heels of his hands.

After nine compressions she bent to seal Alice's mouth with her own, then, pinching her nostrils, she began to breathe down into Alice's lungs. Anna breathed gently but steadily, down and down, then came up to draw in more air and bent again to repeat the manoeuvre—then up, then down once more.

Now Simon was restarting his massage movements; they were counting them together. . . Five. . .six. . .

seven...eight... At that point they heard the sounds of the resuscitation trolley being rushed down the corridor... Nine...ten... And then the resuscitation team piled into the room, sending the door crashing back and connecting Alice to their sophisticated equipment in an attempt to save her life.

At a glance from Simon Anna followed him into the office. 'There's not room to swing a cat in there,' he grunted, sweat beading his lip. Sternal massage was hard work. He looked down at the heels of his hands. 'I felt I was crashing right through her ribs.'

'You probably were,' Anna said shortly, turning to the window. She was disturbed, even upset, but determined not to show it. A nurse wasn't supposed to show anything but calm, not when she was on duty. She had witnessed cardiac arrest before—once during her training years and once only last year, out in a London street.

On both occasions she had wished and willed the patient to survive, but this time the reverse was the case; this time she hoped that Alice's gallant heart would refuse to start beating again; would refuse to pump any more life-blood round her exhausted little body; would decide to remain comatose and give its owner peace.

Still facing the window, Anna looked down into the street. From four floors up the scene below was all but panoramic. In the far distance was the sea-front, teeming with holidaymakers. The sea lay flat and lifeless in the heat, whilst faintly above the rumble of traffic on the main coast road came the strains of the end-of-pier band.

She reached up and closed the window, shutting the real world outside. From inside, from next door, the resuscitation team could be heard in little shifting flurries. There was the slip of their feet on the floor, their muttered voices, the click of equipment, the imperative cry, 'Stand clear' as a shock was directed into Alice's heart from the defibrillating machine. The cry came again, followed by silence.

Simon moved behind Anna's back, and turning round to face him she saw how fatigued he looked. His skin was taut, as though stretched on his bones, whilst the little scar to the right of his chin showed up pearl white— like a paring of fingernail. 'Why don't you sit down? You must have been on your feet all day.' Just in time she stopped herself from laying a hand on his arm.

'I have,' he replied, but he didn't sit down and neither did she. For some curious reason it seemed wrong to take their ease.

A movement at the open doorway showed the pale blond head of Doctor Sven, the anaesthetist, and behind him the rest of the team. They were sorry, they said, they could do nothing more; they had tried, to no avail. After a few words with Anna, who went into the sideward, they drew their trolley back up the corridor— rather more slowly than they had come.

Anna was aware of Simon watching as she replaced one of the pillows under Alice's head, then covered her face. 'Please don't say the obvious,' she all but snapped at him, and added more quietly, 'Thank you for staying, but Jean and I can manage now.'

Obeying her to the letter, he said goodnight and left but it was after six before Anna felt that she could reasonably go off duty. By then Alice's body had been taken down to the hospital chapel at the request of her niece, whom Anna had contacted by phone. Miss Bradbury was Alice's next of kin and only surviving relative. Even so, she made it abundantly clear that she couldn't come that night.

'You haven't given me much warning, have you, Sister? I live three miles out, as you know. I'll look in tomorrow first thing. Meantime, perhaps you could take off her rings and keep them safe. One hears such awful things about corpses being stripped. . .'

'Mrs Fotheringay's personal effects will be taken great care of, Miss Bradbury,' Anna said, forming a mental picture of the hard-faced niece who, according to Jean, had only visited once during Alice's time in the ward.

Whatever must it be like to have no one who cares tuppence about you, she was thinking as she left the colonnade for the scorching heat of the yard. Of course, if you were old your friends might have died, and if you hadn't had any children you could end up like Alice—with no one but a money-grubbing niece, only concerned with stripping off your rings! God, what a thought! And she shivered and felt cold, then told herself to brace up.

She stood for a minute or two, undecided whether to go straight to her car or stop off at the hospital shop for a can of Coke. She could sit down and drink it in the medical school garden, leading off from the shop. She knew about the shop and the garden from Ruth, who had pointed both out to her. If she went there and delayed a little she would miss the worst of Charding's rush-hour traffic and, quite apart from that, she was absolutely parched with thirst. Off she marched to the shop.

It had been built long after the medical school and stuck out from its creeper-clad side like a bare brick appendage, not attractive but functional. As she neared it she could see several of the staff buying evening papers.

Amongst them was Bill Corby. Easy to recognise with his mop of dark curls and short stocky figure, he was still in his surgical coat. With him, and bending his head in conversation, was Simon Easter, the sight of whom halted Anna for a second for she hadn't really banked on meeting either him again *or* Bill Corby that night. Still, to do so was inevitable for they had spotted her and were waiting. She could hardly, with any politeness, turn the other way.

'You've had an action-packed day, Anna!' Bill was the first to speak. 'Thrown in at the deep end, as it were!' His face was the chubby kind.

'It happens!' Anna smiled back at him, whilst on the periphery of her vision she caught the movement of Simon's paper as he tapped it against his thigh.

'I think Sister is probably used to deep ends,' he observed in level tones, not exactly squashing Bill nor praising Anna either. She looked at him then, caught his eye full on her and immediately wished she hadn't rolled up her sleeves or undone the top of her collar. She looked improperly dressed and unprofessional, and was getting hotter by the minute.

'If you'll excuse me,' she said, turning sideways and moving between the two men, 'I'm going to get myself a drink before starting off for home.'

'If you want tea there's the vending machine. . . Cold is at the counter,' Bill called after her, and she raised an arm in answer. Choosing a can of orange juice and taking a plastic beaker from the pyramid on the counter, she pushed through into the enclosed garden at the back of the medical school.

There were one or two students there, stretched out on the strip of grass, but the two long garden seats were free. Taking the nearest one, she opened her can of drink with caution, mindful of her dress, then, stretching out her legs in front of her, she prepared to relax but had taken no more than three sips of her drink when Simon appeared at the shop exit and, to her astonishment, joined her on the seat.

He didn't ask her if she minded, or anything like that, just sat down and half turned to face her, remarking on the brilliant evening and telling her that he was killing time before going up to the station to meet the London train. 'I'm meeting my parents off it; they've travelled from Cornwall today. They're staying with me for a few days before flying off to Corfu.'

'A lovely holiday,' Anna commented, gripping her plastic beaker so tightly that it nearly caved in at the sides.

'A long awaited one, I assure you. My father has just retired. He was a GP in Port Treviss. . .in single practice too. This break is something he and my mother have been looking forward to for goodness knows how long. I'm just glad it's come at last.'

'Will he settle well into retirement, do you think?' Anna asked.

'Well, at first it will be a novelty, won't it?' Simon said thoughtfully. 'How about your folks, are they living near. . .? They'll be younger than mine, of course.'

'Mum and Dad live in Surrey; Dad's a vet.' Anna began to loosen up and talk more naturally. 'He and Prue were in partnership at one time. It was actually Prue's practice then, when she retired and came to live here, Dad took in another partner.'

'Interesting!'

'Yes.' She smiled.

'Your grandmother,' he said, 'is a remarkable lady.'

'You can say that again, and she loves living down here. Her husband, my grandfather, was killed in the War. She was only twenty then and pregnant with Dad. It was fifty-two years ago!'

'She never remarried?'

'I don't think she wanted to.'

He made no comment on that but presently asked her if she knew many people in Charding, apart from the hospital crowd.

'Quite a few, yes,' she said offhandedly, well aware

that she wasn't being strictly truthful but she wasn't going to have him think that she was friendless, or anything like that. Anyway, she knew the Marriners and one or two of her grandmother's friends.

'It's essential, I think, to have a life apart from the hospital—to be able to socialise with people unconnected with blood and guts.' He said this perfectly seriously, not laughing even when she did.

'When I first came here,' he went on, 'my cousin and her husband, who live out at Crowdean, took it upon themselves to get me socialised. At the time I found this irksome; I dislike being ''done good to''. I wanted to concentrate on my job and very little else. Now, however, I find myself looking forward to my free time.'

'Do you get much of it?'

'In a word. . .no!' He did laugh then and bent to pick up his paper, which had fallen from the seat. 'Anna, about Alice Fotheringay,' he said as he straightened up, 'We can't be sorry, can we, that she went as she did? I know everything had to be tried to get her going again, but it was merciful that she switched off and refused to come back again.'

'The last thing she did was smile at us but, like you, I'm glad she's gone. When the team were working on her I actually hoped she'd stay as she was.'

'So did I.'

'She told me I walked like an angel,' Anna smiled, remembering.

'Light, effortless walking. . . Yes, I think she got that right.'

His eyes met hers and something in their depths made Anna's heart beat faster; made her catch her breath and say, looking away from him, 'Alice was a dear.'

'Discerning, too,' Simon said as he got up to go. 'Are you coming now, or staying for a while?' He bent a little towards her, as though about to take her hands and draw her to her feet.

Quickly she reached for her drink, which she'd set down on the seat. 'Oh, I'm staying put, just for a bit; it's called unwinding,' she laughed.

'I hope I didn't spoil the process.'

'Only put it on hold.' Her hands were gripping the beaker, denting the sides again. Then he moved and she began to breathe normally, even managed to reply to his quick 'Goodnight' in an ordinary voice as she watched him walk away.

He was attractive, and he was attracted to her—she knew that without conceit. He had sought her out, and she had glimpsed the sexual interest in his eyes. She was flattered, thrilled—what girl wouldn't be? But she was also on guard. Simon Easter had the power to overturn her life exactly as Daniel had done. She had no intention, *ever*, of going down that road again so it was up to her, wasn't it, to look the other way?

CHAPTER THREE

As ANNA turned into the driveway of The Gables some thirty minutes later it was to see a green Range Rover at the kerb and a small boy in the porch, pulling heads off the clematis and dashing them onto the ground. When he saw her get out of her car he turned to sidle through into the house but she called out to him, darting swiftly across the strip of drive. 'What do you think you're doing?' Her voice wasn't loud, so much as sharp.

He faced her—a slim child in jeans and patterned shirt. 'I'm Tom Marriner, and I'm waiting for my father!' He met her eye defiantly at first and then looked away, pulling at the front of his shirt.

'I see.' So this was Alex's son. 'Why spoil the clematis?' she asked, aware now of a mumble of voices coming from the sitting-room.

'I got bored.'

'That's no excuse, is it?' The voices were getting louder: her grandmother and Alex were coming out. Swift as lightning, Anna stopped and scooped up the severed flower-heads and thrust them into her pocket, noticing Tom go red as she did so—and serve him damn well right.

'Oh, Anna, there you are!' Prue was all smiles. 'Alex has brought me the Japanese prints, and they're exactly what I wanted. . . Fiendishly expensive, of course, but I couldn't beat him down.'

'I'd have Pa to answer to if I brought them down by so much as a penny piece,' Alex said with a courteous firmness, which Anna couldn't help but admire. She admired the way he looked, too—cool on this humid evening in a white cotton shirt and grey linen trousers, with his brown hair brushed smoothly back.

Smiling at her, he introduced his son, pushing him slightly forward. 'Mrs Fellowes is a sister at the hospital, Tom; it was she who looked after Imo, and got her well again.'

'She didn't like it there; she was glad to get home.' Tom's defiant voice was back. 'She has to have all her food taken upstairs—she's not better at all.'

'She'll become better in a day or two, I told you that,' Alex admonished, looking embarrassed and frowning at his son. Don't let him ask the kid to apologise, Anna found herself praying.

But if that was his intention he had no time to carry it out for Prue spoke first, putting a hand on the boy's rigid shoulder, 'Tom's an accomplished horse rider, Anna. He's showing his horse at Collingham this year, Alex has just been telling me.'

'I'm in the under-fifteens class,' Tom supplied, and as he looked up at Anna and smiled she could see the likeness to his father. He had the same vivid blue eyes, the same thin, wide mouth. 'If I pass,' he went on, 'I get a rosette; if I'm the best I get a medal.' His face was flushed; he looked childlike and eager—all his ill-temper had gone.

'Imogen Rayland taught him to ride,' Alex explained. 'She's by way of being a veteran; has been riding all her life. She goes out, now, with the riding school at Haverleigh on occasion.'

'I've got my own horse—a pony,' Tom chattered on. 'She's called Greensleeves; she's got a proper brick stable and a paddock at home.'

'Lucky old her,' Anna smiled, backing towards the stairs. She was longing to shower and change and sit down with something to eat. 'Good luck at the show, Tom; mind you take that medal home.'

'If he does we'll frame it and hang it in the shop.' Alex pulled a face and laughed, moving down the steps with his son, closely followed by Prue. Anna could hear Tom chattering excitedly all the way down to the gate. Alex was silent and walking slowly, seemingly deep in thought.

Prue, as Anna knew, loved children and had a way with them, and a way was certainly needed with a prickly boy like Tom. Even so, he must ride to a very high standard to be competing at Collingham—the biggest and best of the southern agricultural shows. It was held every year, lasted five days and attracted exhibitors from all over England south of The Wash.

Collingham, a small market town some twelve miles north of Charding, became, for those five days, an important meeting-place for farmers, trade and professional people from all walks of life.

Years ago—ten, to be exact—Anna had been to the show herself. She had been seventeen then, and had gone with her parents when on holiday at Charding. It had been her last holiday before starting her training. Her father, she remembered, had volunteered to help with a heifer that had been overcome by the heat.

I wouldn't mind going again, she thought as, stepping out of the shower, she towelled herself, pulling on shorts and a brief bikini top. She was eating her supper by the open window when Prue banged on her door, calling to her through the letterbox, 'Anna, you're wanted on the phone!'

'Who is it?' Anna joined her on the landing.

'Alex Marriner.'

'What on earth would he want with me?' She was totally mystified.

'Well, go down then you'll find out.' Prue, a little puffed, stood aside for Anna to pass, watching her run down the two flights of carpeted stairs and snatch up the phone in the hall.

'Anna Fellowes here.'

'Oh, Anna, hello.' Alex's voice came jerkily into her ear. 'I'm so sorry to bring you down and to disturb Mrs Gatton, but I didn't know your number and of course you're not listed as yet.'

'No, I'm not. . . Alex, there's nothing wrong, is there?' He sounded a bit strained, she thought. Had Imogen Rayland collapsed, or fallen, or suffered a stroke?

'There's nothing wrong, no. . .nothing at all.' There was the merest pause, then he went on to ask, 'Look, I've no idea if this will appeal to you, but Tom and I and Imogen wondered if you'd come to the show with us on Saturday week. That is, of course, if your duty times fit. I expect you sometimes work at weekends.'

Anna was too surprised to say anything for a second; this was the last thing she'd expected. For one thing she didn't think Tom and she had exactly hit it off, and for another she scarcely knew Alex—or Miss Rayland, for that matter. 'It's a very kind thought,' she said hesitatingly, knowing that she was stalling, whilst from the other end she heard Alex say in rather more assured tones:

'Well, think it over; there's no need to let us know at once. We'll be going anyway, starting at ten o'clock and making a day of it.'

'As a matter of fact. . .' Anna made up her mind with a suddenness that surprised her '. . .as a matter of fact I'd love to come. I've not been to Collingham for years, and Saturday week is perfect because that's when I shall be off. . .off duty, I mean. I do alternate weekends, so thank you very much!'

'Good, that's marvellous,' Alex enthused. 'Four is a better number than three and, quite apart from that, Tom and Imogen will be mainly concerned with the equine side of things. You and I can spread ourselves and do a tour of the show. There's so much to see, but I expect you know that. Now, if you'll give me your number. . .' his voice faded as he reached for a pad '. . .I'll ring you nearer the time and confirm when we'll be picking you up.'

'Yes, OK, fine.' Anna relayed her number, then put down the phone, still feeling surprised and, yes, flattered for it would be fun to go out. This would be her first date since coming here, and only a few minutes ago hadn't she been thinking how much she'd like to go to the Collingham Show?

Prue called her into her sitting-room to show her the two Japanese prints that Alex had bid for at auction, and she made no bones about asking Anna why he had telephoned. When she heard why, she looked pleased. 'You'll enjoy yourself,' she said, but made no further comment, seeming far more interested on deciding where to hang her prints to get the best effect.

Back in her flat Anna reflected that in going to the show with Alex and Tom, and Imogen Rayland, she would be doing precisely what Simon had advised— socialising with people who had nothing at all to do with hospital life.

Next day she saw him in full regalia, heading a teaching round. She and Jean had warning of this soon after the hand-over session, and immediately after breakfast they were busy getting case-notes and X-rays in order, getting charts made up to date, ensuring that the results of laboratory investigations were attached to mount sheets and assembling any equipment which might be needed during the round.

In the middle of all this Miss Fotheringay's niece arrived and asked to see Anna, Mrs Johnson's young husband came to take his wife home, and three middle-aged patients admitted for dilatation and curettage were admitted and shown to their beds. They were due, Anna knew, to be 'prepped' in turn and would go off to Theatres, starting at half-past nine. 'Bill will be operating,' Meg told her, 'and I will be assisting.'

At three minutes past ten exactly Simon appeared in the office doorway, six young medics—two males and four females—ranged behind him.

And no one, but no one, Anna thought, wishing them all good morning, could take him for other than a senior consultant—not simply because he wasn't wearing a white coat but because in any garb he would exude a presence, a manner and bearing. . .all this, aside from his charm.

He was approachable too, and informative; he wasn't the sort to make students squirm for the hell of it, nor be lofty with ward sisters, as some of the senior doctors were.

At his request she outlined each patient's case history for the benefit of the students and, as they proceeded from bed to bed, they were invited to ask questions and in some cases—with the patient's permission—carry out routine checks under Simon's vigilant eye. The more seriously ill patients weren't disturbed, their conditions being discussed well away from the bedsides—up at the nurses' station.

Mrs Tooley was perfectly happy to tell them all they wanted to know. 'You can 'ave a butcher's at what-ever you want, not that there's much to see. I've 'ad everything taken away, you see, but they tell me it's all for the best.'

'You'll be a new woman, Mrs Tooley.' Simon watched Anna cover her up.

Karen Miller, now safely pregnant, minded nothing at all but that fact, and she knitted industriously all the time her operative details were discussed. At the end of it she thanked Simon again for what he had done, promising him *and* Anna a slice of christening cake.

The round proceeded slowly and by the time it was over, and the students had dispersed to the medical school, it was time for ward lunches. Simon was in the office with Anna, signing prescriptions, when his bleeper made its plaintive squeaking. As he reached for the phone she heard his curt, 'Easter here,' after which there was a second of silence before he snapped out, 'OK, coming now.' He slammed down the phone and muttered, 'Acute abdomen. . .A and E,' as he strode up the corridor.

'I was just bringing this.' Rosina, the domestic, appeared with two cups of coffee. 'Sister Hilton always gave Mr Easter coffee.' She looked reproachfully at Anna, as though it was all her fault that he'd gone rushing off.

'No matter—' Anna took the tray from her '—I can drink both cups. With the amount of talking I've done this morning I'm as dry as a husk.'

'I expect you mean dehydrated,' said Rosina, who fancied herself as a nurse.

The luncheon trolley was trundled into the ward before Anna had finished her coffee. She and Janice Hall served out the food—salads for those who were extra health-conscious, cottage pie for those who were not. There was only one NIL BY MOUTH sign this morning—over the bed of Miss Ida Drew, who was to have a cone biopsy later that afternoon.

The three D and C ladies, back from Theatres, were still half-asleep. Anna gave orders that they were not to be roused; they could have something later on.

Once the last portion of raspberry jelly and ice-cream had been handed out she went up to her own lunch, returning to find Meg in the office with details about the A and E admission.

'It was an ectopic gestation. Simon decided to have her prepped in Cas and taken straight up to Theatres. She presented with generalised abdominal pain and signs of internal bleeding. She's a Mrs Cotton, she's twenty-eight, and all I've got so far are her GP's letter and cross-matching details. She'll be on transfusion so best have her in the main ward, don't you think? Miss Rayland's bed would be ideal, being next to the nurses' station.'

'It's the only one free,' Anna said, 'till the D and C patients go home. There are three admissions for Sunday, too.' She was looking at the list.

'Aye, it never stops, does it?' Meg went into the ward to see Mrs Tooley and Mrs Jacobs, the fibroidectomy.

Fay Cotton, having been stabilised in Recovery, was brought up to the ward at a little before four o'clock when teas were being served and most of the visitors were leaving, carefully replacing chairs and stools under the central table and staring at the stretcher trolley as it was wheeled up the ward.

Anna supervised Fay's transference to the bed, and bent to speak to her. 'You're in the ward now, Mrs Cotton. I'm Sister Fellowes. I and my nurses are here to look after you; just relax now and sleep.'

Fay tried to smile. She had green-hazel eyes which opened wide for a second, the pallor of her skin accentuating the freckles over her nose. A transfusion line ran into her left arm, whilst on her right one above the elbow was a sphyg. cuff, deflated and unconnected, to allow her blood pressure to be checked at intervals without disturbing her.

Observing the level of the blood bottle and checking the flow rate, Anna left Jean in charge and half an hour later went off duty, still thinking about the young woman who, without surgical intervention, would most certainly have died and might still do so. She did her level best to put that pale, freckled face out of her mind, without much success.

It was all very well for nurses to be indoctrinated with the concept of being detached but sometimes this was difficult to follow, and possibly even Simon found it to be so for next morning Anna was told that he had paid a midnight visit to Fay, just to make sure that she was all right. He had discontinued the transfusion, and a blood specimen had been sent to the labs who reported that her h.b. was up to 12 g per 100 ml.

'Brilliant!' Anna said to Meg when she came to do her round, 'I mean, when you think what she was like yesterday.'

'It's the surgeon who's brilliant.' Meg handed the lab report back to Anna for mounting in the notes.

By the time Simon came up to the ward, during the late afternoon, Fay was well enough to ask him herself exactly what had been done. 'Oh, I know I shall be all right,' she said. 'Sister's assured me of that, but will the operation I've had affect my chances of having a family later on? I didn't so much as *suspect* I was pregnant this time round—I simply thought my curse had stopped because I was run down. Then, when the pain started and I felt so grim, I was sure it was appendicitis.'

'The symptoms and pain are similar, Mrs Cotton—' Simon was taking her pulse '—and, in answer to your query, I can see no reason why you shouldn't have a family later on. What happened this time was that your egg embedded itself in your left-hand tube, instead of sailing on to your uterus and making its home there. As it grew the tube ruptured, causing much bleeding, so I had to go ahead and remove it—there was simply nothing else to be done.

'The good news is that on the right-hand side you have a healthy tube and ovary, all you need for starting off again once you're fit and well.'

'Thanks, I'm relieved—' she plucked at her sheet '—although at the moment I feel completely anti the idea; it's my husband who wants a child.'

'Yes, well, you've had a rough time,' Simon said guardedly, 'and you've still got a little more blood to make up, you know. The transfusion has given you a good kick-start. Eating up your greens and good nursing care is bound to do the rest.' He smiled at her and she smiled back but, then, thought Anna, who wouldn't? Who could help responding to his charms, even if your h.b. level was still two points down and even if your insides grated like teeth every time you breathed?

He went off to see the D and C patient who was being kept in for further tests and investigations and possible surgery. Jean Ross chaperoned him this time, as Anna was called to the phone to deal with an anxious relative, who would speak to no one else but her. The call took some time and when she'd finished Simon had left the ward. 'You'll no be seeing him till Monday,' Meg said, putting her head round the door. 'He seldom comes in at weekends unless there's an emairgency.'

'I dare say I'll live,' Anna laughed, feeling relief—spiked with an annoying disappointment—wash over her.

*   *   *

As it happened, though—or as fate decreed it—she was to see him on Sunday, and not at the hospital either but down on the beach.

It was a spur-of-the-moment decision that sent Anna down there for a swim at eight in the morning before starting her 'lates' shift at twelve. It was the first Sunday in July, and a hot one, so why not make the most of it before the hospital walls enclosed her again? Slipping a sun-dress over her bikini and collecting a towel, a Mars bar and her beach-bag, she walked down the road to the sea.

If she had anticipated having the beach to herself she couldn't have been more wrong. It wasn't crowded and it wouldn't be for another hour, she knew, but there were several bobbing heads in the water, and little bundles of towels and discarded clothes were lying around on the stones. There was a family having breakfast, complete with spread cloth. One or two of the promenade shops were pulling out their awnings and beach chalets were being unlocked. The day was unfolding itself.

Stripping off her dress and standing for a minute in her black and white bikini enjoying the kiss of the sun on her skin, Anna stepped over the shingle and plunged into the water, gasping at its chill. But once submerged it was blissful; heaven to be lifted like a feather-weight by the incoming swell, then swept down into its valley of glass-mountain smoothness and up on the other side.

How lucky she was to be living on the coast; how lucky she was to be able to relax like this; to have the sea practically on her doorstep—a mere distance of two roads away.

She struck out away from the shore, then turned and swam parallel with it. From so far away the people on the beach looked like marionettes. Exhausted at last, she turned on her back, letting the water take her, floating and staring up into blueness and emptying her mind of everything but the here and now—the sun, and sea, and the sky.

Some fifteen minutes later she turned for the shore and swam in, scrambling quickly upright before her knees hit the sand. It was when she was wading through the surf that she spotted the man sitting by her beach-bag—a long-limbed man in denim shorts and T-shirt, a man who got to his feet in one light springing movement as he saw her approach.

With a feeling of shock she recognised Simon and was immediately conscious of the way she must look to him as she emerged from the sea, half-naked and streaming with water with her hair plastered down like a cap. 'Fancy meeting here!' was all she seemed capable of saying.

'Why so surprised?' He came forward to help her over the bank of shingle. 'It's the nearest bathing beach for both of us, and if we both like an early dip, which clearly we do. . .' He smiled at her easily, watching her pick up her towel.

'It's heaven in the water.'

'I know; I've been in. I rent one of the chalets.' He gestured back to the line of little 'houses' with their green roofs and red front doors. 'I was just getting dressed when I spotted you striking out for Dieppe!'

'I'm a strong swimmer.'

'I could see that.'

Her face emerged from the towel, dry now and slightly flushed, her hair already beginning to shade to its customary red-gold and arrange itself in curves.

'Is this your weekend off?' he asked, and she shook her head.

'No, it's not. I'm on duty at twelve; I'd better go and get dressed.'

'Join the contortionists, you mean?' He glanced over towards the breakwater, where one or two bathers were trying to dress beneath towels which kept slipping off.

'Well, at least I shan't be alone,' Anna laughed, and was about to say goodbye and walk away when he thrust a hand in his shorts and pulled out a key.

'Look I've just thought,' he exclaimed, 'why not use my chalet? Come with me and I'll unlock it for you— it's a little stiff to turn.'

She hesitated and was about to refuse, for she didn't want to get closer to him, did she? Then she thought how stupid that was. Borrowing his chalet was innocuous enough, and far more dignified than wriggling under an inadequate towel. It would be downright rude to refuse. So, 'Thanks,' she said, 'that's very kind.'

'Not at all; it makes sense.' His tone was brisk. They began to walk up the beach, clish-clashing over the shingle to the lower promenade, where he unlocked the door of chalet nine, and left her to go inside. 'I'll wait for you here, by the sea wall,' he told her, 'but don't rush; you've got plenty of time.'

The chalet smelled of wood and sand, and faintly of seaweed. It was very tidy, with two folding chairs stacked under a bench. There was a square of mirror above the bench and a high strip of window over the door, which she could only see through by standing on tiptoe. When she did so—when she reached up—she could see Simon by the wall, lean and long in his shorts and T-shirt, sandals on his feet, his hair lion-coloured and thick, lying close to his head.

She looked away quickly, drying herself, pulling on briefs and sundress and combing her hair in front of the mirror with a hand that trembled slightly. Of all people to run into down here—just when she had resolved to meet him only as Mr Easter-the-Consultant and never as Simon-the-man.

'Damn and damn,' she muttered to herself, but that wasn't how she felt. What she was feeling was anticipation, and she cursed herself for a fool.

When she opened the door he came forward to lock it, taking the key from her hand. 'All right?' he enquired.

'Very much so; thank you again.' She started to move away from him more determinedly this time, even managing to get her tongue round the sensible word 'goodbye'. But perhaps she didn't say it loudly enough, or perhaps he wasn't listening, or was resolved not to take any heed, for the next thing she knew he was saying that he'd see her to her car.

'I expect, like me, you've left it in The Lion yard,' he said.

As he bent to pick up a ball and lob it back to a boy on the beach, he heard Anna say, 'I've not brought the car—it seemed a good idea to walk.'

'In that case. . .' he dusted sand from his hands '. . .I'll drive you home.'

'Oh no, there's no need!' She felt a pang of alarm. 'There's no need; I've got oceans of time!'

'Splendid, then we'll take in coffee as well. I know just the place,' he said pleasantly, beginning to turn towards the ramp.

'But there won't be anywhere decent open; it's still not nine o'clock!' She had walked right into that one, she realised. . .talking about oceans of time.

'I said I knew just the place, Anna.' His hand came warmly round her arm. 'I meant my place, Andover Square; that's decent enough, I think. We could have coffee in the garden and then I'll whisk you home afterwards.'

He was taking charge; and with a suddenness that

surprised her she let him carry on. It would be pretty silly, anyway, to turn his invitation down. It would only amuse him, or amaze him—or both—and what possible harm would it do to have coffee with him in his garden? 'It sounds a lovely idea,' she said, and they continued up the ramp.

The car was the same as she remembered it from Tuesday—deep and luxurious. It was he who was different—casually dressed, the sun showing up a dusting of fine gold hairs on his arms as he reversed out of the yard.

She was intensely, disturbingly aware of him, so much so she could hardly draw breath. And under it all she despised her own weakness for what on earth was she doing, allowing herself to stay in his company when she should have been walking home—increasing the distance between them and not running the risk of getting to know him better, which she knew was dangerous?

CHAPTER FOUR

SIMON's house, as he'd said, was very like Prue's, Anna saw as they stopped at the kerb. It had iron railings, though, instead of a hedge, and no front lawn—just a paved run-in for the convenience of his patients who would need somewhere to park.

She noticed the gleaming brass plate to the right of the front door—SIMON V. EASTER, FRCS. FRCOG. 'Mrs Gill,' he said, locking the car, 'polishes that plate with metal polish and TLC every single day.' He opened the door, letting loose an elderly terrier with a rough brindle coat, who ran to Simon, making whining sounds in his throat.

He bent to fondle the dog.

'Have you eaten this morning?' he asked.

Anna shook her head.

'Then you can manage some toast. I can't eat alone, and I happen to be ravenous.'

'Well, in that case, thank you.' Her hair hid her face as she looked down at the dog, who growled at her and backed away, showing his teeth.

'Mind your manners, Buzz!' Simon told him off. 'He takes time to get used to strangers,' he explained. 'He's one of the wary kind.'

Simon shut the dog back in the house before escorting Anna up the sideway and into the back garden, which was a surprise when compared with the front.

'Do you approve?' he asked, his eyes on her face.

'I certainly do!' From the patio on which he seated her, she looked down at the sloping lawn, at the herbaceous borders flaring with colour, at the rose-beds and lily pond. The enclosing lichened stone walls, which were pleasing to the eye, were of just the right height and stoutness to afford protection against the gales.

'I'll show you round properly when we've eaten.' Simon disappeared to get the tray of food before coming back to say, after pouring the coffee and passing Anna toast, 'I inherited from my predecessor John Duran his private patients, his nurse/secretary, and Buzz.'

'Buzz? Oh, of course, the dog. But fancy leaving him behind!'

'I suppose it was understandable in the circumstances, you know. John and his wife were emigrating, and as Buzz was elderly they didn't think it fair to transport him to the other side of the world. They arranged for James Petersen, the ENT surgeon, and his wife to take him in. They live just opposite here, and they dote on dogs.

'So over the Square went a perplexed little dog but he was very soon back again, barking at the kitchen door until someone let him in. After a month of this the Petersens and I did a deal—Buzz became mine and came back to his home, which had been his plan all along! He's fourteen now; we're used to one another, and he's not alone all that much. My daily, Mrs Gill is here every weekday until five, and I'm home very soon after that.'

'I hope he doesn't growl at your patients.' Anna spread honey on her toast.

'He's not allowed near the front door, nor up in the consulting-rooms. He knows his place; he's been well trained. Miss Benson, my secretary, would throw a fit if he so much as breathed up the stairs.'

'Did you mind having a built-in secretary?' Anna asked, after a pause.

'If I'd minded seriously we'd have had to part,' Simon

grunted. 'I wouldn't say we're the perfect team but Amy knows the work from A to Z and she's loyal too, if a trifle condescending. After working for John, who was in his late sixties, she looks upon me as a learner consultant which, in some respects, I am.'

'Medical people learn all the time, however young or old they are,' Anna said stoutly, thinking what a cheek the Benson woman had.

'True.' Simon refilled her cup, and a little silence fell, but not an uneasy one. Sitting there, looking down on the garden in the company of this man whom she'd once thought resembled Daniel, Anna was aware of an inexplicable warmth that was nothing to do with the sun.

'Tell me,' he spoke so suddenly that she gave a little jump, 'last Tuesday, when I barged into your office, why were you so shocked? I don't usually make *quite* such an impact—' his grey eyes twinkled '—so am I right in thinking that you mistook me for someone else?'

'Yes, I did. . . For my. . .for Daniel.' Anna set down her cup. 'I'd been thinking about him a few minutes earlier, then you came in and although you're not like him, not feature by feature, you're the same physical type—tall and fairish—and for a second or two I thought I'd conjured him up!' She laughed as she spoke, but not very naturally. He remained serious.

'I'm so sorry.'

'Not your fault.'

'You must miss him.'

'Yes.'

Another silence fell between them, a far less comfortable one—twanging with unasked questions on his part, and determination on Anna's not to divulge or let slip one single thing more. She wished she hadn't lied about Daniel—about saying that she missed him—for she didn't, not any longer, not in the way that Simon assumed. She drank her coffee, draining her cup, and even that tasted bitter. Desperate to break the silence, she enquired about his parents. 'Did your parents get off all right—on holiday, I mean?'

'They did, yes.' He sat back in his chair, folding his arms. 'I ran them to Gatwick last night, both of them thrilled at the thought of three weeks' idleness in one another's company. They'll be celebrating their ruby wedding in Corfu.'

'Forty years of marriage!' Anna's voice held a note of awe.

'More than most couples of our generation are likely to *want* to achieve. Most find the marriage state fettering; it's not for everyone. I, for instance, was glad to get out of it.' He swiped at a wasp and missed.

Pity you ever got in it, then, Anna was tempted to retort, and what about his wife? Had she felt fettered, or had she been left desperately and frantically wondering where she'd gone wrong? She felt angered by his attitude, his *male* attitude. No wonder his marriage had failed. 'Have some more coffee,' he was asking her, and she felt that he was closing the door on further talk about marriage, and a good thing too.

'Thank you, but no.' She half rose. 'I ought to be getting back.'

'Of course, and I'll take you. . .' he unrolled himself, and stood up beside her '. . .but first let me show you my consulting-rooms; I'd like your view of them.'

Best-quality flannel, she thought, still feeling ruffled on behalf of all womankind. Still, she couldn't be rude to him here in his own house, and he couldn't have known that his comments on marriage were such a sore point with her.

His rooms were attractive, airy and light, even welcoming. There was nothing dark and looming and

gloomy, not even in the examination area with its couch
and trolley and glass-fronted cabinets. The pictures on
the walls were of country scenes; there were vertical
blinds at the windows. In the secretary's office a fuschia
in a pot graced one of the sills. There was a word pro-
cessor too, Anna noticed, as well as a fax and a copier.
'Does your secretary work full time?' she asked, going
over to look at the plant.

'In hours, yes. She works six half-days, sometimes a
little more. I see patients in the early evening and on
Saturdays; I need her to chaperon then.'

'Do you ever have to cancel appointments—I
mean because of the hospital, if there's an emergency
admission?' She walked back to his side.

'Occasionally, yes, but not often. Bill Corby's a tower
of strength, but if it does happen Miss Benson has to do
what she can to stop a patient arriving or placate them
if they're here. She was a theatre sister at the Regent,
you know, till she had a skiing accident about ten years
ago and injured her back, which put paid to a standing
job. She's close on sixty now, but doesn't want to retire.'

A mature nurse/secretary. Anna took this in, a curious
feeling of light-hearted relief taking hold of her. She
commented again, almost fulsomely, on the pleasantness
of the rooms as Simon held the door wide and she passed
through to the landing and stairs.

'They weren't like this when I took over,' he was
saying, but got no further for, before his eyes and without
warning, Anna was crashing down on the floor, whilst
a yelping, hysterical Buzz went streaking down the stairs.
'*Anna. . . Anna!*' Simon swooped to lift her up but she
was already scrambling to her knees, and managed—
without his help—to get to her feet, breathless and
shaken, pushing her hair off her face.

'Buzz. . . I fell over him. . . Is he all right?'

'Never mind about Buzz. Are *you* all right?' He held her upright, his hands on her upper arms.

'I'm fine, just fine.' And now she could laugh. 'Good thing you've got a soft floor!'

'What a fright you gave me, "disappearing" like that!' He sounded as shaken as she. He was still holding her arms, but differently, his hands moving up her shoulders and inwards to her neck under her bell of hair.

His touch was mesmeric, spellbinding, magic. She stared at the blue of his shirt, at the curve of his throat rising out of it, at his jaw and the curve on his mouth which was bending to hers and speaking her name softly, like a breeze. 'Enchanting Anna,' she heard him whisper.

Buzz came back, eyed Anna with suspicion and made his way over to Simon, who told him he was lucky that it wasn't Amy Benson he'd sabotaged. 'She hasn't got fall-resistant bones, nor a very forgiving nature!'

'I'm not so sure that *I* have,' Anna laughed, pointing out that if she didn't leave at once and make tracks for home, she'd be hauled in front of the SNO for being late on duty. 'And that, believe me, would be a far worse fate than tripping over Buzz.'

They spoke little on the short drive round to Romsey Road. Simon seemed to be deep in thought, or was probably concentrating on the Sunday traffic—which was rapidly building up. As for Anna, she was still reacting from the way she'd felt in his house—standing on the landing so close to him, his hands smoothing her arms. Never, not since Daniel, had she felt so attracted to a man; so impelled to be close; to touch and be touched; attracted enough to agree to whatever he asked.

She closed her eyes, shivering a little. She must take a good grip on herself. He was the wrong man; he was the too-charming kind, the non-staying kind. She knew all about that sort, didn't she, and what about all those resolutions she'd made to be on her guard?

As they pulled up outside The Gables she hoped that Prue wasn't about or she'd ask Simon in for certain sure, but a swift glance showed the front garden to be empty. Thank heaven for that. 'Well, here you are, all safe and sound—bar a bruise or two, perhaps.' Simon was being jocular, yet sounded anxious as well.

'Thank you for breakfast; it came just right.' Anna moved to unfasten her seat belt.

'I enjoyed your company.' His voice sounded near and, as her belt went slithering back, she felt his gaze and heard him say, 'Will you come out for a meal with me one evening when we're both free? We'd have more time then and, with the long, light evenings, we could drive out a little way.'

'Oh!' the expletive shot out of her, whilst the startled thoughts in her head assembled themselves into two opposing sides. Tell him yes, one side urged; tell him you'd love to go. Whilst the other, with an even louder voice, urged her to turn him down.

'It would be fun, Anna, and we all need a little of that in our lives,' Simon's voice intruded gently, which was when she made up her mind.

'It's kind of you, Simon, but I'd rather not.' She made herself look at him. 'You see, I think what you said the other evening about it being best to go out with folk unconnected with the hospital is very true. We need a change from day-to-day hospital faces, we both of us do.'

'Well, well!' His expression was one of surprise and stiff amusement. 'So you're making me eat my words, Sister Fellowes!'

'If you like, yes, I suppose I am,' she managed to smile at him.

'And you're right, of course.' He half turned to open the door on his side. Getting out onto the pavement, he walked round the front of the car—tall, lithe, brown-limbed, *male*. Anna's mouth went dry. He had taken her *congé* so lightly. Didn't he mind at all?

Gathering up her beach-bag, she got out of the car the second he opened the door. Standing in the roadway facing him, standing front-to-front, there was just a moment when it looked as though he might ask her again; when she might have, just might have—almost certainly *would* have—said yes to anything, but the moment passed, as moments do, and all he said as he escorted her safely to the pavement was, 'Thanks for your company,' and left.

Hearing him drive off as she let herself into the hall, hearing the car's powerful engine growing fainter and dying away, gave her an excluded, lonely feeling—like standing behind a closed door.

By the time she had got to the hospital, however, and was walking onto the ward, willowy trim in her uniform, doing her round of the patients, the morning's events—whilst not forgotten—had slipped back into second place.

Sunday afternoon on the ward was different from other days. There were more visitors, for one thing, and some brought children who, as Meg Brodie said, were a flaming nuisance, dancing all over the place.

Meg was on the ward to take clerking details of the three new patients, who were due for surgery on Tuesday. One, a young woman who was fourteen weeks' pregnant, was to undergo cervical cerclage. Her stay would be short—maybe only one night—but the two older ladies, each with troublesome fibroids, might be in till the end of the week. As always, every bed was taken and the nurses were at full stretch.

Anna was concerned about the D and C patient kept back for further surgery. She knew that Simon intended to operate during the afternoon of Monday. Miss Barton, who was forty-eight, looked after her arthritic father. She was worried about him being without her, even though the medical social worker had told her that he was having round-the-clock care.

'She thinks no one can look after him as well as herself, which is just plain daft,' Meg said, jutting her lip, and Anna couldn't help but agree.

'I just hope she won't decide to discharge herself.' She looked through the viewing window at the irresolute Angela Barton, who was talking to her elderly visitor— a schoolteacher like herself.

'I'll ask Bill to have a word with her.' Meg finished her tea. 'She's not likely to be in long, though, not more than three or four days—although I expect she'll be back for radiotherapy, depending on what Simon finds.'

In the end it was Simon who had a word with her early next morning. He found her calmer than he expected, and no longer all of a jump. She was perfectly happy, she told him, to undergo surgery but in no way...*no way*...would she come back for follow-up treatment. 'You do your best for me, Mr Easter; after that I'll take pot luck. I made up my mind to that at three o'clock this morning.

'No, please don't waste your valuable time—' she smiled at him over her glasses '—trying to persuade me otherwise; it won't do a scrap of good.' And she didn't exactly wave him away but there was, nevertheless, a distinct air of dismissal about her manner and the way she spoke.

He didn't look particularly pleased, either, as they turned away from the bed. 'Well, let's just hope that the tumour hasn't spread to surrounding tissues,' he said a little grimly up at the ward desk. 'The signs are that it hasn't, which is why I'm going to do a vaginal hysterectomy and save her the pain of an abdominal wound.

'Now, while I'm here—' he glanced up at the clock '—I'll check on Mrs Tooley. We need her bed, and she's due for discharge. Can you produce her notes. . .at the double, please, Sister? Right now I ought to be downstairs, getting scrubbed up.'

'Of course.' Anna got the notes from the office. Then quickly, but not at the double, she joined him at Mrs Tooley's bedside, slipping back the single sheet that covered her so that he could examine her wound. After asking one or two questions, he authorised her discharge.

'You can go home tomorrow, Mrs Tooley,' he smiled, and sat down on her bed. 'A community nurse will call to take out your stitches at the end of the week. You'll feel a lot more comfortable then, but you must take things very gently till you return here for your outpatient's appointment in six weeks' time. Sister will make an appointment for you, and give you a card.'

'Thanks ever so, sir.' Mrs Tooley's creased little face went pink with pleasure. 'My Stan'll be pleased to 'ave me back; he's missed me, bless his 'eart.'

'*We'll* miss you,' Simon said, dead on cue.

'I bet you say that to all the patients.' Mrs Tooley's eyes rested admiringly on his broad shoulders as he turned to go out of the ward. 'Good-lookin', 'ent he, like them doctors on telly? Sexy too, I'll be bound.'

'Lucky old him.'

Anna trailed in his wake but he didn't turn into the office, just raised an arm and called back to her, 'Got to be on my way!'

'Short and sweet today,' Jean Ross grinned, coming out of the linen room.

In time *and* manner, Anna thought, returning to the ward to do a last-minute check on the vulvectomy patient before the porters arrived with their trolley and theatre canvas, and poles, and their cheerful comments of, 'Soon be done now, luv' and 'We'll soon be bringing you safely back to bed'. She supposed the patients drew comfort from this, although the pre-med drug had usually done its work by then—inducing a state of languid euphoria which was hard to penetrate.

It was Friday before Anna saw Simon again, and by then she had acquired a brand new learner nurse straight from Introductory Block. Her name was May Fenn, and she was thrilled to be on the gynae ward. 'I thought it might be male medical,' she said, 'all spewing up into cups.'

Whatever else she lacks it's certainly not confidence, Anna thought, watching her making beds with Nurse Cheng, her sturdy 'milk-bottle' legs planted wide apart in the way she'd been taught so as to safeguard her back. She believed in asking questions too, and on going to the top—which was Anna—for the answers.

'What's cervical cerclage mean?' she asked, catching Anna in the office on Friday morning when she was checking her stock of drugs.

'Well, it literally means—' Anna relocked the cupboard and pocketed the keys '—encircling the cervix with a tape suture to straighten and narrow it up. This prevents the developing foetus from dropping through too soon. In the ordinary way it wouldn't do so, but in Mrs Drew's case she had too rapid a delivery with her previous pregnancy and her cervix was traumatised. The suture will stay in until she's thirty-eight weeks, then be taken out ready for labour.'

'What a *good* idea!' May Fenn's eyes practically came out on stalks.

'Yes, I suppose you could say that.' Anna tried her hardest not to laugh.

'It's like tightening the sleeve of a sweater, isn't it?'

'An apt simile!' said a voice from the doorway. May turned round to see who it was. Anna turned too, but out of politeness for she knew who was there. She knew it was Simon; she would have known his voice amongst a hundred others. At a word from her, May scuttled off to help Janice with mid-morning drinks, whilst Simon, entering the office, perched on the end of the desk. 'An apt simile and a good explanation—clear and to the point.'

'Thanks.' Anna moved to shut the window against a sudden downpour of rain. This afforded her time to hide her pleasure at his praise.

'Do you like teaching?' He was clearly in less of a hurry than usual.

'I don't mind it when I've got the time—' she turned round and faced him '—and when the pupil is bright and enthusiastic, as May Fenn certainly is.'

He nodded, saying nothing, and her eyes dropped from his. He had a disconcerting way of looking at her, not staring exactly but observing closely—making her feel like she was on the end of a pin.

'How can I help you?' she asked formally, meeting his eyes at last.

'Ah, yes, of course, to business.' He unhitched himself from the desk. 'Miss Barton and Mrs Drew can, I think, take leave of us tomorrow so perhaps we could go in and see them, and I'd like a squint at their notes.'

Anna produced the two sets of folders and went with him into the ward. Miss Barton was in the day room, playing Scrabble with Mrs Curry, the vulvectomy patient, who moved about gingerly—wary of her drainage bag. Miss Barton was examined back on her bed and 'signed off', as Simon called it. 'You've done splendidly, Miss Barton.' He closed her notes with a snap.

'You mean *you* have,' she corrected. 'I haven't done very much, apart from keeping my fingers crossed and laying down the law.'

'Your tumour wasn't invasive; it was simple to get it away,' he said, thankful that this was so, and that he could look her in the eye.

'But tell me,' she said, and this time it was her gaze fixing his, 'if I'd been willing, would you still have prescribed cytotoxic treatment?'

'No, I wouldn't have,' he said, emphatically. 'That's not the way we work. Treatment where no treatment is necessary does more harm than good. Don't forget your follow-up appointment, though, will you, in six weeks' time?' She assured him that she wouldn't, thanked him again and went back to the day room—to Mrs Curry, and the Scrabble board, and her cup of cooling coffee.

Mrs Drew was eating a Mars bar, sitting by her bed in a pink dressing-gown with her long black hair tumbling down her neck. She was very pretty, thrilled to be pregnant and dedicated to chocolate. Laying a hand on her as-yet flat abdomen, she got to her feet, looking faintly alarmed at the sight of the great man himself. 'Is everything all right?' she asked, dropping back on the chair again.

'Couldn't be better, Mrs Drew,' Simon assured her quickly. 'You've no discomfort, have you, no dragging, or colicky pain?'

She shook her head with emphasis. 'Can't feel a thing. The worst was the anaesthetic.'

'Well, in another four or five weeks—' he watched Anna helping Cynthia Drew on to the bed '—you'll be feeling your baby shifting around.' He began to examine her, palpating her lower abdomen with the flat of his hand. His expression was one of total absorption.

He was always, Anna had noticed, a little remote at

such times—all but on a different plane. And she knew
the reason why, of course, for, especially in a gynae
ward, the patients were extra-defenceless; embarrassment for most was less than skin-deep, and he respected
this—he even deferred to it. Jokes on the gynae ward
were taboo, and quite right too.

'No can do,' he said back in the office, when Anna
suggested coffee. 'I have to attend a meeting with my
peers at eleven, called by one of the financial managers,
to discuss the distribution of funds. I want Gynae to have
its fair slice of the cake.'

'Of course,' Anna said, taking Cynthia Drew's notes
from his hand and catching his smile before he turned
and went out of the door, disappointing Rosina yet again
as she came out of the kitchen with coffee and biscuits
and a slice of Genoa cake.

'He always stayed in Sister Hilton's day. Perhaps you
don't tell him *soon* enough,' she said by way of accusa-
tion, dumping the tray on the desk.

Jean came in to share it with Anna, reporting that they
were running short of drawsheets—there were only four
left—and did Anna know that Mrs Day had been smoking in the loo again, and Mrs Jacobs was complaining
that her breakfast egg wasn't one of the special free-range
ones which her husband had brought in for her.

Anna sorted out the drawsheet problem, had a tactful
word with Mrs Day about her smoking and promised
Mrs Jacobs that she'd mark her eggs with a cross so that
she'd know she'd got the right ones.

After this she welcomed the new patient who was
taking Mrs Tooley's bed, supervised the ward lunches,
went up and had her own, had a word with Janice Hall—
who was still set on leaving—and at the start of visiting
talked to Fay Cotton's husband—a hectoring, florid-

faced man—who demanded to know when he and his wife could try for another child.

'I'm keen to have a son, and as soon as possible,' he said in the kind of tone normally used for ordering a sofa or a sack of boiler fuel.

Inwardly outraged, but hiding it, Anna asked him to sit down. 'Mrs Cotton is making a good recovery,' she told him quietly, 'but a tubal pregnancy is a serious condition, especially when—as in her case—there has been a considerable loss of blood. Mr Easter hasn't given any indication yet as to when she'll be discharged, and even when she's home it will be some time before she's really strong.'

'This isn't what we planned.' He looked annoyed.

'I don't suppose it is,' Anna said with restraint, wanting nothing more than to push her fist into his jowly, frowning face.

'I'd like to see her surgeon, this Easter fellow; he's never here when I come.'

'Well, he doesn't actually hang about, Mr Cotton, on the off-chance of seeing relatives, but I'll certainly tell him that you'd like to see him, then I'll ring you and let you know when.'

'That's the best you can do, is it?'

'At this stage, I'm afraid it is.'

He rose from the chair, hitching up his trousers which—because of his acorn shape—had a tendency to slip to his scrotal region and have to be jerked up. He was considerably older than his wife, Anna thought, probably by twenty years, which might account for his selfish rush to beget a child. Feeling a little sorry for him—but even more sorry for his wife—she watched him huff his way into the ward, looking up and down it in an overseeing kind of way before walking along to Fay's bed.

Weatherwise, it was a mixed sort of day—the sun blazing out one minute, rain gushing down the next. By mid-afternoon it was mostly rain and Anna began to fear for her date with Alex next day at the Collingham County Show.

He had rung her twice during the week to confirm starting times, and to reiterate how much he was looking forward to it all. He was the kind of man, Anna decided, who didn't like anything left to chance, and she could sympathise with this for she was tidy-minded herself, liking to plan ahead and look forward—not do things all in a rush.

It was not only raining when she went off duty at a little after four but coming down in torrents, whilst thunder—as yet far off—clattered thinly over the Channel, which was streaked with violet-blue. Stepping out of the crowded lift, she spied Simon by the exit doors amongst little knots and groups of visitors waiting to take the plunge out. He was giving every indication of making a dash for it.

Almost involuntarily seeking his company, Anna made for the doors as well—just as one of the hall porters thrust an umbrella into his hand. 'Might as well use this, sir, it's going spare.'

'Oh. . . Thanks.' As he turned he saw Anna. 'You off home?' he asked.

'Yes, I am.'

'Then you'd better share this; no sense in getting drenched.' The doors parted as he approached them and kept wide as she passed them as well. He had the umbrella up with one quick thrust and drew Anna under its shelter, keeping his free hand under her elbow as they set off across the yard.

It was a large, black, enveloping umbrella and it sheltered them like a roof, withstanding the hard pelt of the rain, affording privacy and inducing a kind of intimacy too—making Anna feel protected, and cared for and warmed right through to her bones. She wouldn't have minded if her car had been two miles away; she didn't notice the splash of rain round her legs, drenching her up to her knees.

She was oblivious to all and everything but Simon— the clasp of his hand round her arm, the brush of his thigh against her own, and the up-and-down sound of his voice as they half walked, half jogged, towards the parking lot.

'Good thing I saw you—' his breath came in jerks '—or you'd have got very wet.'

'An act of pure gallantry.' She was breathless too.

'Oh, so that's what it was!' His hand tightened on her arm, but now they had reached her car. Low, yellow, gleaming and washed, it seemed to stand out with annoying signalling brilliance, as though determined not to be missed.

As she bent to unlock it and as she swung the door open, he stood there sheltering her. All she needed to do was dip down into the driving seat, switch on the engine and say goodbye—but she did none of these things. Instead she turned round to thank him, meeting his eyes head-on for a fleeting second before he bent forward and kissed her on the lips.

Even without his arms around her it was a very positive kiss—a link, a message, a foretaste of bliss—and its swift, meaningful pressure was alive on her mouth, like a gentle madness, as she drove the car thoughtfully home.

CHAPTER FIVE

'TOM listens to Imogen far more readily than he does to me,' Alex confessed to Anna in the tea marquee next day. They were at the Collingham Show; had been there since eleven; and at three o'clock had watched Tom putting Greensleeves through her paces in the under-fifteens event.

There had been twelve competitors who, one by one, had been weeded down to two—Tom and a girl called Paula Felde on a magnificent blue roan, which she'd handled with confident skill. She was older than Tom by five years but, even so, there had been little to choose between them, and Anna had found herself very nearly as tense as Alex, as time and time again the two had been asked to canter and trot their horses in front of the judges' stand.

But Paula Felde had been proclaimed the winner and tumultuous applause had rung out. She had gone up for her medal, followed by Tom who'd had a rosette pinned to his jacket. He, too, had got his share of applause but, instead of acknowledging it, he'd ducked his head and made straight for where Alex, Anna and Imogen were sitting. There had been congratulations from all three, and from people sitting nearby, but his small face had been stormy as he turned it to his father.

'It should have been me,' his voice cracked. 'I was the best; I know I was; the judges just liked her horse!'

He was close to tears and Anna found herself feeling sorry for him. It had been a close thing, very close, and the strain must have been enormous for a little boy who was not quite nine years old. Alex bent to him and talked to him quietly.

'You rode superbly well, Tom, and there wasn't much difference between you, but the judges' decision is final; you can't get away from that. Paula Felde is a lot older than you; she's had more experience. What you must do now is go back down there and congratulate her. Don't let people see you're a bad loser, that's no way to go on.'

Tom shook his head and looked mutinous, 'You must be joking!' he cried, pushing past his father and Anna to get to Imogen. '*You* could see I was the best, couldn't you, Imo. . .? You could see it wasn't fair?'

She persuaded him up on the seat beside her, but what she said to him was inaudible to Alex and Anna as the loudspeaker was blaring out details of the next event. It was plain, though, that she'd made him see reason for straight away they saw him going back down the gangway and along to the front of the stand where Paula Felde was talking to a reporter and having her photograph taken.

Tom approached her and proffered his hand, which she shook with enthusiasm, and then he was coming back through the tiers of the stand, pink-cheeked and pleased with himself. 'The newspaper man said I was a real trouper, and *she* said I ought to have won!'

'Good lad.' Alex made room for him on the seat but he took his place beside Imogen again, and sat there throughout the show jumping and the following dressage event.

Soon after five, when they were thinking about tea, Imogen excused herself. 'I think I'll make my way home, Alex.' She looked tired and a little drawn. She had travelled in her own car to the show in order to be at the ground when Greensleeves arrived in her box and, by the same token now, she wanted to be at home to stable the mare when she got back. Tom elected to go with her, so off they went—the grey-haired woman in her blue suit and the small, striding boy in sleek riding habit, hard hat under one arm.

'So, it's just us for tea,' Alex said, which was how he and Anna had come to be in the marquee together, talking about Tom.

'Has Miss Rayland been with you since he was very young. . .since your wife died?' Anna asked with care, but feeling that Alex wanted to talk.

'She came to us when he was five. He'd just started school. She was House Matron at a prep school for boys at Bayford, along the coast, saw our advert for a house-keeper, decided she wanted a change and came to us— just like that. We couldn't believe our luck. We still can't; she's a treasure and wonderful with Tom, who isn't easy, but I can't help wishing he had more time for me.'

Perhaps you don't try to share his interests, Anna thought but didn't say, confining herself to asking how Tom did at school.

'He's top of his form, good at sports too, but he likes to win.'

'Most of us do,' Anna laughed and, relieved when Alex joined in, she ventured to say that it could just be that at the age Tom was now he responded more easily to a woman. 'I couldn't help noticing how he opened up to my grandmother when you came to The Gables last week.'

'So he did to you,' Alex was quick to say.

Anna wasn't so sure, but she nodded and said, 'Maybe,' and shortly after that they went on to talk of other things, culminating in Alex asking her if she'd mind visiting Mapleton and Company's stand.

'The fine art dealers?' She was interested at once.

'And auctioneers. Yes, that's right,' he smiled back at her, well pleased. 'I do quite a bit of business with them, both in London and here. They suggested I should call on them; they're keeping open house at their stand.'

Anna did a quick mental résumé about what she was wearing. Would a short linen skirt, a multicoloured shirt and hair loose about her face pass muster at the Mapleton stand, which might easily, she thought, be entertaining moneyed clients all in correct country clothes? She had noticed their stand when they'd first arrived; it was built like a small bungalow. 'Perhaps,' she said uncertainly, 'I ought to tidy up a bit first.'

'You're fine as you are,' he said, looking at her with the cool eye of a man used to appraising beautiful things.

Reassured, she reached for her bag. 'In that case, ready when you are.' Instinctively she realised that he set great store by appearances. He, himself, in a light flannel suit and Turnbull and Asser shirt, looked prosperous and well-turned out, and if he hadn't considered that she complemented his image he would never, she knew, have asked her to accompany him to the toffee-nosed Mapleton's stand.

He's a perfectionist; he'd be hard to live up to but, even so, I like him; I like him a lot, she was thinking as they left the marquee and came out into the sunshine again.

It was five-thirty and more and more people were pouring in through the turnstiles. After the fiasco of yesterday the weather had decided to behave itself. There was just enough breeze to flutter the bunting and put snapping life into flags and awnings, and to give coolness to the cattle in their makeshift shelters and pens.

The atmosphere wasn't unlike a very 'upmarket market'. Groups of people met other groups they hadn't seen for a year. There were hoardings everywhere advertising cattle-feed and dips and special treatments for ticks. There was a smell of hay, of trodden grass, of oil from the columns and lines of farm machinery being demonstrated—in striking contrast to the magnificent shire-horses pulling an old-fashioned plough.

Somewhere over by the children's funfair the band was playing the Oompa-pa tune from *Oliver* as, side by side with Alex, Anna walked onto the veranda of Mapleton and Company's stand.

The three rooms into which it had been divided were peopled with chattering businessmen, some with their wives but most without, and a hired waiter was serving drinks. Alex was hailed—in fact, descended upon—by the senior partner, a smiling, bald-headed man in his sixties who ran the London, Mayfair office. He knew Alex well and was charmed, he said, to meet a friend of his. He plied them with refreshments, although Alex refused champagne.

'Anna and I want to get home in one piece tonight,' he joked. Anna had a glass and felt better for it with every passing minute, and perhaps it was partly the champagne that made her accept, with no hesitation at all, Alex's invitation to have dinner with him one evening. He broached this on the way home, showing pleasure when she said yes.

'We could try that new restaurant at the top of the Grand Hotel—I've heard one or two people speak well of it.' He flicked a glance at her as they turned off from the roundabout onto the main Charding road.

'I'd like that,' Anna enthused, pushing out of her mind the thought that less than a week ago Simon had invited her out and she'd made herself refuse. But Alex is easier, different altogether, not a threat to my happiness, she told herself, hearing him suggest Tuesday evening, to which she agreed.

She wouldn't have minded him kissing her when they got back to The Gables, but she didn't long for this to happen and neither was she surprised when all he did was grip her hands tightly, then slide back into the car.

He's not the sort to sweep a girl off her feet, she thought, letting herself into the hall, but he's attractive and I like him; passion isn't all. Without warning again, and annoyingly, Simon slid into her mind just as Prue came in from the garden, brandishing the evening paper.

'Anna, there's been a baby abandoned. . .at the hospital. . .in Casualty! There's a photograph. Look—' she stabbed a finger at the bottom of the front page '—there's your Mr Easter holding it. The poor little thing was left there, they think, early this morning, and only a few hours old!'

Wordlessly Anna took the paper from her grandmother, and stared at the blurred photograph of Simon standing with the child in his arms. He could have been anyone, with his face half-turned, looking down at the shawled bundle. He was wearing a white coat, which Sister Rose Webb would have insisted he donned whilst up in the baby unit—she was a stickler for would-be germs.

'A newborn baby boy,' Anna started to read, 'was left in the casualty department of the Regent Hospital today in a plastic bag, wrapped in a towel and crying lustily. Mr Simon Easter, Consultant Gynaecologist, pictured above, said the baby appeared to be in good health, but appealed for the mother to come forward as she may be in need of medical care. It is emphasised that no charges of any kind will be brought.'

'It was on the six o'clock news as well,' Prue said, pushing Anna through into her flat. 'A nurse was holding the baby then, and there was a picture of the ward.'

'I expect the nurse was Rose Webb, the sister on

Maternity.' Anna handed the paper back. 'Let's hope the mother turns up, but I'd like to bet she won't. We had a case like that at the Walbrook once.' She sat down heavily on Prue's settee, feeling deadly tired. Champagne, when long gone, leaves lassitude in its wake, and she very nearly snapped at Prue when she asked her if she was going to ring Rose Webb up.

'No, I'm certainly not,' she said. 'She wouldn't thank me for it; she'd think I was muscling in, stealing her limelight! I'll go up and see the baby on Monday, if it hasn't been claimed before then.'

'You nurses are a funny lot!' Prue pulled a face.

'A breed apart.' Anna managed to laugh and to go on to talk about the show, and about Tom being runner-up in his event and getting a rosette.

'Not the medal, then?' Prue looked concerned.

'No, a girl got that.'

'Was he very upset?'

'I'm afraid he was, and he couldn't hide it at first, but Imogen Rayland had words with him—what they were I don't know—but they did the trick; he went off and congratulated the girl, much to Alex's relief *and* mine. I thought there'd be a scene. Anyway, she, Imogen, took him home afterwards so that they could see to his horse. Alex and I had tea together, then went on to Mapletons' stand.'

'*The* Mapletons. . . Wowee!' Prue liked to use what she thought of as modern expressions.

'Alex was welcomed like royalty.'

'That surprises me not at all; the Marriners move in exalted circles; their business is top of the tree.'

'I suppose it is.' Anna got up to go.

'And you enjoyed yourself, I hope?'

'Yes, I did, more than I thought I would. It was such an utter change.'

'Good.' Prue switched her radio on. 'I'm very glad to hear it. It's time you began to go out and about, and meet lots of interesting men.'

Anna was on lates on Monday, getting to the hospital at midday, but before she'd even reached the lifts she learned that the mother of the abandoned baby had come in for treatment. Not having time to learn all the details, she hurried up to Gynae and along to the office, where she found Simon deep in conversation with a tawny-haired man in glasses. Both swung round at her approach.

Jean was there too but, relieved to see Anna, she hurried away, whereupon Simon introduced the stranger as James Petersen, ENT consultant, adding, as they shook hands, 'And this is Mrs Fellowes, James, our new ward sister.'

Why is he here? was Anna's first thought, then learned that Fay Cotton, the ectopic patient, had developed an infected throat. 'I regret to say she has acute streptococcal tonsillitis, Sister.' James Petersen looked with undisguised pleasure at Anna's lovely face.

'She's been moved into number two side-ward to prevent droplet infection,' Simon put in tersely. 'The last thing we need is the whole ward going down with it. I suppose she picked it up from one of her visitors?' His expression was grim.

'She may well have done so, but we can't check on everyone who comes through the doors.' Anna looked vexed. 'But it's a great pity, just as she was doing so well; she seemed particularly well when I left here on Friday night.'

'Respiratory infections can manifest themselves very quickly,' Petersen said, still staring at Anna as though at a mirage. 'I've suggested spraying her throat with amethocaine hydrochlor. . .better than gargling, which won't reach the whole inflammatory area and may increase her pain. Give her lozenges to suck—they'll increase her saliva and prevent her neck stiffening up.

'I'll see her again tomorrow. . .sooner if you're worried.' He was talking mainly to Anna, walking backwards towards the door, then as he bumped against the jamb he said, leaning slightly forward, 'Didn't I see you at the Collingham Show on Saturday, watching the riding events? You were on the same side of the ring as me. . . with that handsome husband of yours.'

'Not my husband—he's dead. I was there with a friend,' Anna replied, a little more crushingly than she'd intended, aware as she was of Simon moving impatiently at her side.

'I was certain I'd seen you somewhere before and then remembered that it was here, but we'd never been introduced, had we?' Petersen's smile flashed out once more.

'No, we hadn't.' Anna willed him to go—there were new patients to see, there was the report to be dealt with and she wanted to ask Simon about the abandoned child.

In the end it was he who got Petersen moving by all but nudging him out, thanking him so fulsomely as he did so that his tactics went unobserved. 'So, you enjoyed your weekend, did you?' He turned back to Anna again.

'Very much.' She moved to the desk, feeling more in charge, as well as more divided from him, behind its solid bulk.

'The Collingham Show is well worth a visit. I went to it last year.' He lifted a globe paperweight, balanced it in his hand and then set it down, waiting silently as though hoping to be told more. Instead, seizing the opportunity, Anna asked him about the baby.

'They told me in Reception that the mother turned up, so is everything all right?'

'Depends—' Simon's expression was grim '—on how you look at it. The kid's still upstairs in Maternity, abandoned yet again. Neither his mother nor his outraged grandmother want to recognise his existence.'

'Then the mother's gone home?'

'She needed suturing but was otherwise OK and, yes, she went home after breakfast today—as happy as Larry, according to Sister Webb who's exploding all over the place.'

'Was she a teenage mother?'

'Eighteen, name of Dawn Payne. Her mother insists that she didn't know Dawn was pregnant.'

'But that's ridiculous!' Anna exclaimed. 'Of *course* she must have known!'

'Not necessarily,' Simon corrected. 'Dawn is a very big girl, obese even—like her mother—which can mask a great many things. Mrs Payne works in London and is away all day, so hardly sees the girl. *She's* unemployed and just drifts around, which is how she got pregnant, no doubt. She doesn't know who the father is, says ''it was a party job'', had no antenatal care whatsoever and just hoped ''it'' would go away.'

'Good Lord!' Anna was still trying to get her breath.

'In the event, she gave birth at a friend's house in the small hours of Saturday. The friend, whom she won't name, dumped the child here several hours later.'

'But. . . Was it all right?'

'Messy. . .wrapped around in a duvet cover. It. . .or rather ''he''; let's humanise him, poor little devil. . .was still attached to his cord with the placenta lying on his chest. According to Mrs Payne, the first she knew of it was when Dawn arrived home at lunchtime on Sunday and fainted on the step. She brought her here straight away, which at least showed common sense.'

'But she didn't want to see the baby... It was her grandchild, for heaven's sake!'

'She refused to see him; Dawn wouldn't look at him. So far as they are concerned, he never happened. Unless Dawn has a change of heart, which is very unlikely, he'll come up for adoption in due course after a period of fostering.'

'How was it,' Anna asked, still taking all this in, 'that you were involved? I didn't think you were usually here on a Saturday.'

'Quite right,' he said, 'I'm not, but I was called in to an RTA victim with pelvic injuries. I was in Casualty when one of the paramedics spotted the bag, heard the baby wailing and brought it to me when I was washing my hands! There was a fair bit of excitement and commotion for a time.'

'I can believe it.' Anna pictured the scene and then, returning to matters a little nearer home, asked if the pelvic injury patient was in the gynae ward.

'No, in Intensive Care, but later on today she'll be transferred to one of the ortho wards, where she'll also be attended by Eric Salter's urology team. She has bladder injuries, along with a crushed pelvic ring.'

'Poor woman,' Anna sympathised, but she was nevertheless glad that she wasn't being transferred to Gynae, which would almost certainly have meant putting off one of the patients due to be admitted that week.

'A weekend's respite vanishes like sea mist once you're back in harness, Anna,' Simon observed, looking beyond her through the window into the ward. She was about to ask him if he wanted to see anyone in particular when he said that he had to go and did so, talking about returning later on.

With the ward lunches out of the way, and the quiet hour begun, Jean came in to deal with the hand-over report, ending with details of the five new patients who had come in the day before.

'Nil by mouth for all of them as from midnight,' she said, 'except Mrs Spry for conization—she's last on the list. It's a hell of a business about Fay Cotton, isn't it. . .? Difficult too to get her to take enough fluid, although a straw seems to help. Her throat is absolutely raw, poor love; I feel so sorry for her. Come to that, I'm sorry for *us*, having the chore of barrier nursing on top of everything else.'

Sighing theatrically, she returned to the ward, followed shortly by Anna, who wanted to do her round before visiting began. Afterwards, slipping on a gown and mask, Anna went to the side-ward to see Fay.

She was propped up high, looked flushed and unhappy, and had pushed the bedclothes down as far as her waist, her thin arms lying limply at her sides. 'Don't. . .want. . .visitors,' she croaked at Anna. 'Not Nigel. . .or anyone.'

'Don't worry, I'll make sure no one comes in,' Anna said, taking Fay's pulse and looking at her charts, noting that her temperature had risen to over 102. No wonder the poor girl felt ill. Leaving her to rest and assuring her again that no visitors would be allowed in, she left the room to wash her hands, take off her gown and mask and deploy the nurses on their various tasks, including the learner, May Fenn who—eager as ever—was put in charge of Fay Cotton's obs.

After visiting was over Meg Brodie arrived to do her round, together with an anaesthetist to check over the patients due for surgery next day. The phlebotomist came to take blood for cross-matching and Bill Corby looked in on Fay. Pretty soon it was ward suppers and then evening visiting.

Along came Nigel Cotton with a long, stiff sheaf of

salmon gladioli, carrying it into the ward like a poker and stopping short when he failed to see his wife. Anna, who was in the ward talking to Mrs Curry, went forward to meet him, telling him what had occurred.

'*Tonsillitis*! Do you mean to tell me she caught it in here, in hospital, where everything is supposed to be germ-free?'

'No one knows how these things are caught, Mr Cotton. Your wife could have contracted it from a visitor, or even one of the staff carrying the virus but not actually developing it. I think perhaps—' Anna strove to be tactful '—it might be as well if you didn't go in to see her this evening—it's difficult for her to talk.'

'Where is she?' He looked momentarily floored.

'In one of our side-wards; she's being kept comfortable.'

Expecting a scene, Anna was relieved when he turned on his heel, said he'd come back in a day or two and made off at speed with the air of a man who suspected that germs were chasing him out of the doors. It was unfortunate that, in his haste, he forgot to leave the flowers. Still, I can tell Fay he's been, Anna reasoned; I can even lie in my teeth, say that he sent his love and best wishes and not mention the flowers at all.

Two other visitors wanted to see Anna but there were no real problems and at half-past seven, during her own supper break, she found time to slip up to the maternity wing to see the abandoned child.

The visitors in the postnatal ward were mainly proud fathers, and one or two young-looking grannies were craning their necks over cots. Rose Webb was off duty but the midwife in charge, who had been told that Anna might come up, brought the baby out of the nursery and placed him in her arms.

Sitting down with him in a small room leading off the

nursery, Anna was unprepared for the wash of emotion
that swept over her. Not that the baby was beautiful—
he was wrinkled and shock-haired, his head came up to
a point and he was pale with spots on his chin.

But it was his vulnerability that got to her—the feel
of him in her arms, his warmth and small bulk through
the Babygro that the nurses had found for him. 'How
could anyone turn their back on you; leave you here like
this? How could your mum want to be rid of you?' she
whispered, close to his face.

She was so engrossed in baby worship and in battling
with her feelings that she was unaware of anyone entering the room until she saw Simon, squatting on his heels
in front of her, his eyes level with hers.

'I thought you might find time to visit.' His forefinger
stroked the child's cheek.

'Then you were right, weren't you?' she said briskly,
unwilling to let him see how holding the baby affected
her. Why did he have to come up just then?

'The nurses are calling him Little Pete.' Simon was
standing up. All she could see of him were his legs and
front and the edge of his suit jacket. 'Do you approve?'
he asked, and now his voice was way above her head.

'Oliver would be better. . . He looks a forlorn little
chap,' Anna replied and, as if agreeing, the baby started
to yell. Crooning to him she lifted him and held him
against her shoulder, whereupon his wailing ceased as
he settled himself and curled his head in her neck.

'He's taken to you; sensible chap,' Simon said, and
was just in time to see the look on her face and the start
of tears before she got to her feet and bore the baby
back to the nursery, laying him in his cot.

'I know how you feel, Sister.' The midwife had seen
her distress. 'I cried buckets when he was brought in—
all the time we were cleaning him up. Still, shows we're

human, doesn't it. . .? Blow this talk of being detached. I'll tell Rose you've been, and come up again, if you want to, at any time.'

Composed once more, Anna left the unit, relieved to find that Simon was nowhere to be seen, as she went through the corridor doors. He was waiting for her at the head of the stairs, though, and in no way could she escape. 'He'll be all right, you know,' he remarked as they descended to the gynae floor. 'A couple longing for a child will adopt him, and he'll be spoiled rotten all his life. The natural mother isn't *always* the best person to look after her child.'

'I realise that—' her voice was muffled '—but, to be honest—' she turned and faced him as they reached the landing '—I was upset for myself. It was that old nuisance, the maternal instinct, manifesting itself!' She laughed, feeling better; there was nothing like facing the truth and stating it too.

But Simon didn't, however, laugh with her, and he was grave-faced as he said, 'You'll remarry one day, Anna, and have children of your own.'

'I intend to,' she said quietly, 'but in the meantime I've a ward to get back to. Are you coming in, or were you just. . .?'

'Off home,' he finished for her, turning and making his way towards the lifts.

Much later, in bed that night, she wondered why she had answered Simon in the way she had, for to say that she intended to marry again implied either that there was a man in her life wanting to marry her, or that she was actually hunting for one. . .neither of which was true.

CHAPTER SIX

CONVERSATION flowed easily between Anna and Alex during their dinner date at the Albermarle Restaurant on top of the Grand Hotel. The view from its windows was breathtaking—eight miles of curving coastline, the sea faintly pink, reflecting a sky which had recently slipped its sun.

It had been another hot day and the streets and promenade—even the clifftop grass and beach—were still exuding warmth. Aloft in the cream and gold restaurant, however, there was welcome, drifting coolness from the open sliding windows, like patio doors, which let in the hiss of the sea.

Anna had felt a tremor of uncertainty as she'd showered and dressed earlier on. Did she really *want* to go? What had she let herself in for? Did she want to know Alex better, and where would it lead to if she did? She zipped herself into a cream silk dress with not too plunging a neckline. A topaz necklet, matching earrings and the new-penny gleam of her swinging newly washed bob, caused heads to turn when she and Alex were shown to their banquette table just before eight o'clock.

He was the perfect host—attentive, interesting. They discovered that they liked the same sort of food, films and books, and also Arthur Pinter's seascapes—a local artist, who'd died ten years previously. With all this behind them in mutual sharing, it didn't seem too strange, nor too intrusive, when Alex asked her the same question that Simon had two days before, although leading up to it rather more carefully.

'Do you still miss your husband, Anna,' he said, 'or have you adjusted to widowhood?'

'I still think of him but, yes, I've adjusted.' She watched him refill her glass.

'Would you marry again, if the right man came along?'

'Like a shot!' she said and laughed, then tempered this by adding, 'Yes, I would like to remarry and I hope to, eventually, but I'm in no hurry. I'm enjoying the present and, of course, I love my job.'

'You have youth on your side; you don't have to worry.'

'I'm not *that* young. . .less than three years off thirty, which is a milestone in a woman's life. Anyway, what about you,' she ventured, 'are you going to plunge again?'

He looked away from her unsmilingly and, with a little pang of alarm, she wondered if she ought to have phrased the question a little more delicately. He's not the kind of man you can bounce things at; he likes to be prepared for what's coming, she thought, sipping the last of the claret they'd enjoyed with their saddle of lamb.

'If I could find someone who would share my interests and come to love my son, yes, I would certainly marry again,' he said, looking down at his plate and moving a piece of cheese onto a cracker with careful meticulousness. 'Two years ago I thought I had met her, but. . .' he put down his knife with a little click and pushed at his plate '. . .she made a fool of me, a complete fool. And that sort of thing. . .' he turned to Anna again '. . .makes a man careful next time round.'

'Of course. . . Oh, how awful! Alex, I'm so sorry. . .' she began, then broke off because he was looking beyond her, further up the room, raising his hand and smiling. . .

Following his eyes, she saw no one she knew, and he quickly explained that he'd spotted a friend of the family... 'She's Pa's goddaughter, as a matter of fact, name of Julia Trafford. Looks as though she's sporting a new man; Julia's a great one for change. They must have come in at the far end through the cocktail lounge. That's her, look, near that yucca plant, wearing a jade dress.'

Intrigued, Anna looked and spotted Julia Trafford without too much difficulty. She had dark, piled-up hair and an expanse of creamy skin was well in evidence above the neckline of her dress. She didn't look all that young, though; she was probably, Anna thought, well into her thirties—not that it was easy to tell in this light, and from a distance of twenty yards or so.

She was talking to the waiter, who was inclining towards her and hiding her escort from view, and as he moved—all but bowing from the table—Anna's heart leapt for she was looking...she was looking at Simon, sitting there straight and tall, unfamiliar and oh so attractive in a dinner jacket, his head turned towards the girl.

Anna's feelings were in turmoil. How dare he...how dare he sit there, like that, with *her*...? How could he even want to when he's been as he has with me—even asked me out? Yes, but you refused him didn't you...? You turned him down. And what a good job I did because even if I hadn't he'd still have been here with her! He *is* like Daniel, very much like Daniel. For that's what he would have done...*did* do, time and again. I'm *glad* I turned him down!

She, that woman—that Julia Trafford—was talking and moving her hands. Perhaps she was pointing Alex out to him for the next minute they were looking down the room, and the occupants of both tables were acknowledging one another with smiles and little waves. If Simon was surprised he hid it well; his mouthed 'hello' to Anna was relaxed and, cheerful and unselfconscious, he was out to enjoy himself. No doubt, Anna seethed thickly, he was anticipating the joys of slipping into bed with the creamy-skinned Julia after their sumptuous meal.

'Do you know the man she's with?' Alex was watching Anna's face.

'I ought to.' She took a grip of herself. 'He happens to be the consultant gynaecologist at the Regent. I see him most days. As a matter of fact he's the surgeon who patched up Imogen.'

'Really?' Alex's eyes flicked to their table again.

'Yes, really, really!' Anna gave a strained laugh, hearing him say,

'Julia's rarely without an escort, and they're usually professional types. She's a doctor herself—a research scientist in the field of equinine disease. She's made a name for herself world-wide, and often lectures abroad. Her father and mine have been friends since their university days.'

'She sounds clever,' Anna said, very nearly adding, brains as well as sexual charms, but stopped herself just in time. They were touching glasses, she noticed, and once again something akin to pure outrage washed over her, making her want to get to her feet and shout and throw something heavy. She must be out of her mind.

'Would you prefer,' Alex's mild-toned voice infiltrated her ire, 'to have coffee here at our table, or through in the lounge?'

'Actually,' she told him longing not only to get out of the restaurant but out of the hotel and off its environs before she boiled up again, 'I don't think I've got room for coffee, after such an enormous meal.'

'Same here.' Alex's napkin joined hers on the table-top. 'I often skip coffee at this time of day.' He was looking about for the waiter who, seeing his signal, brought their bill on a plate. 'I don't think we need to stop off and speak to Julia and your friend—unless you particularly want to, that is?'

'No.' Anna shook her head. 'I know how I'd feel if someone barged in just to say hello when I was out on a date, especially if I was eating. It would put me off my food.'

Alex laughed. 'There'll be other opportunities for you to meet Julia,' he said as the waiter eased their table away and they left the restaurant. Walking slightly ahead of him, Anna wondered what he meant. Surely he wasn't going to suggest a foursome... What a gruesome thought!

A taxi bore them to Romsey Road, waiting at the kerb whilst Alex saw her up the path and into the shadow of the porch. His goodnight kiss was the light, swift kind but his arms about her back held her in the way she liked, making her feel happy and good about herself and taking the painful edge off the recurring image of Simon with Julia in the Albermarle Restaurant.

Over the following three weeks Anna and Alex began meeting on a regular basis. Not surprisingly, owing to Charding lacking the anonymity of London, they were seen around by colleagues and friends who coupled their names and who gossiped, and wondered, and whispered, and assumed—in the way that people do.

This was brought home to Anna one morning on the ward when Rose came down from Maternity to borrow some paper sheets. Rose and Dick Painter from Rheumatology had seen Anna and Alex at the theatre the evening before.

'We noticed you were in the best seats,' Rose grinned. 'Nice to have a rich fella!'

'I go out with Alex because I like him, not because he's rich. I'm no gold-digger,' Anna called down from the top of the ladder in Clean Utility, where she was reaching for the sheets.

'Still, I bet he takes you to some fabulous places. How did you come to meet him. . .? You haven't been here that long.'

'Actually,' said Anna, descending the ladder with a good deal of care. 'I knew Alex *before* I came here; I've known him quite some time.' This was stretching the truth and she knew it, for she had only met him once— just before she'd taken up her job—when she'd bought Prue's jug. Still, it would give Rose something to think about, and to spread about as well.

'Oh, I see, I didn't *realise*.' Rose looked intrigued but, on getting nothing further from Anna, thanked her for the sheets and made for the doorway, only to find it blocked by Simon, who stood there, a hand on the jamb, looking in at them.

'You'll find Bill in Maternity, Sister Webb, waiting to do the round,' he said with a little edge to his voice, and Rose went off at a trot.

The utility room was just inside the doors leading out to the lifts, so he must have heard what we were saying, Anna realised, and this was confirmed when he said with little embarrassment and even less subtlety, 'I hear that your friend, Alex, would like to get married again.'

Anna got her breath back with difficulty, 'Yes, so he tells me,' she said. Julia Trafford would have let that slip, she was sure; she might even have hinted, for good measure, that she, Anna, might be in the running.

'He has a son, I believe?' Simon's face was inscrutable.

'A super little boy,' Anna said, with her tongue in her cheek and a smile on her face to cover the false description, for Tom was a child from hell. 'Perhaps we should get on,' she added, holding onto her smile with difficulty and aching muscles. 'Have you come to do a full round?'

'No, only the latest post-ops, the two hysterectomies due for discharge and the perinotomy,' he said without smiling at all. 'I'll only need Mrs Cole's notes and perhaps the Pearson girl's, and I'm running late so if you wouldn't mind hurrying,' he had the cheek to add as he entered the ward, leaving Anna to stop off at the office to pick up the notes and to get rid of May Fenn, who was hanging about by the desk.

'Later, May,' she said, as the girl asked her what 'anastomosis' was, please, and did it mean joining up ends?

Simon was waiting, arms folded, at Mrs Cole's bedside. At little more than twenty-four hours post-op she thought she should be helped out of bed, and kept on and on about it. She had had an ovarian tumour removed as big as a full-term baby. She had a large wound and a lot of stitches, and she was eighty-one years old. Simon didn't want her mobilised for another full day.

'Tomorrow, maybe,' he was telling her as Anna caught up with him. 'You'd find it very uncomfortable moving about today.'

'Painful, you mean. . . Oh, I don't mind that; I can put up with pain. What I don't want is to drop dead from a clot, long before my time.' She had thick grey hair, which the pillows had pushed up in a bush all over her head—this and her eyes, bright with fever, made her look fighting fierce.

'We won't let that happen, Mrs Cole.' Simon was gentle with her. 'You'll have breathing exercises this morning from Miss Gunne, our physio. She's a dab hand at preventing clots. Meantime, I'd like you to rest.'

'I hope she won't be long.'

'She won't,' Simon promised, as they left her bed. 'Well, there's a first time for everything,' he remarked at the ward desk, 'but I don't think I've ever before known a patient so anxious to be up and about.'

'Certainly not at such an early stage,' Anna agreed, glancing back at Mrs Cole, who, with her head stuck rigidly forward, was anxiously watching the doors. 'Strictly speaking,' she added, 'she should have gone into Geriatrics.'

'I prefer to have her here,' was Simon's reply, and Anna said no more.

The two hysterectomy patients were checked and their discharges agreed for that afternoon, which delighted both ladies who made for the pay-phone to telephone their families.

Jill Pearson, the perinotomy patient, was a young woman of nineteen who had recently moved in with her boyfriend and was encountering sexual difficulties, due to a narrow introitus. Simon had performed a midline episiotomy long enough to provide an adequate vaginal orifice.

She had soluble stitches in place, which were giving her pain on movement. 'We'll keep you in another day, Jill,' Simon explained, 'then you can go home, and as each day passes the discomfort will grow less. Once it has completely gone, in about two to three weeks, recommence intercourse to prevent the new opening shrinking down.'

'All right.' She looked faintly embarrassed, and wisely Simon said no more beyond assuring her that many young women had the same trouble as she.

'Otherwise we'll be having her thinking she's a freak,' he said to Anna at the doors, then hurried away to a meeting with one of the paediatric team.

The consultant paediatrician, Paul Gee, was the doctor who had pronounced Baby Payne fit and well, and sanctioned his release to foster-parents ten days ago. His mother and grandmother never came back to the hospital to see him. 'They've washed the poor little kid right out of their lives,' Rose said as she folded up his blankets with a murderous look in her eye.

By lunchtime, when Mrs Cole had made two near-successful attempts to get out of bed, Anna decided that cot-sides were the only sensible step. It was difficult, if not impossible, to watch her all the time—especially as they were one nurse short, due to Janice Hall having left.

Nurse Cheng was sent to get the cot-sides out of Stores. 'But don't bring them in until I've had a word with Mrs Cole,' Anna told her, putting down her pen and going to sit by the old lady's bed. 'Mrs Cole, we feel your bed is a little on the narrow side,' she began, 'and, in case you fall out when you're asleep, we thought we'd put some rails up—little chromium bars, like pipes, which will keep you perfectly safe.'

'Do the other patients have them?' Mrs Cole looked suspiciously round at her near neighbours and across the aisle—not a rail to be seen.

'Some do, yes. The beds all vary a little in width.' Oh, what terrible lies, Anna thought, keeping her fingers crossed. 'In your case it really is necessary. We wouldn't like you to fall.'

By sheer luck her last sentence struck the right note. 'I did fall out of bed once, at home,' Mrs Cole confessed. 'I sort of rolled, and the next thing I knew there I was on the floor. So, do what you think is best, dear,' she conceded gracefully, making no protest when, a few minutes later, the sides were slotted in place.

The afternoon brought its usual spate of visitors, one of them being Jill Pearson's boyfriend who came in bearing carnations and fern. The two hysterectomy ladies went home, effusive in their thanks for everything that had been done for them as they were wheeled out to the lifts. At teatime Miss Tell, the SNO, rang through to say that an agency nurse by the name of Shirley Dobson would be starting on the ward next day.

Anna had just put the phone down when, through the viewing window, she saw Simon in the ward. . . But he was coming out. . . Seconds later he was at her door.

'Why cot-sides on Mrs Cole's bed?' he demanded, not raising his voice but looking as though he would like to, his grey eyes glittering like glass.

'Because she kept trying to get out.' Anna shot to her feet. 'I haven't got enough nurses to watch her all the time, and she's got this fixation about clots!'

'You seem determined to treat her as senile!'

'That's not the case!' Just in time she stopped herself telling him that he was talking rubbish.

'Cot-sides are bad psychologically!' He came further into the room.

'So is falling on the floor and seeing your insides decorating the vinyl!'

'I very much doubt if that would have happened.'

'I didn't, and don't, intend. . .' Anna paused to catch her breath '. . .to put it to the test, and I prepared Mrs Cole before the sides were brought into the ward. Tomorrow, when she's less demented and when I have an extra nurse, she'll be able to sit out of bed for a time, which will satisfy her, I hope. In which case the cot-sides, which are psychologically damaging, can go back to Stores.'

Simon's mouth opened to deliver a broadside—of that Anna was sure—but right on cue Rosina appeared in the doorway with a tray of tea. 'Just managed to catch you in time, Mr Easter,' she said, all unaware of anything amiss till he turned on his heel and left without a word.

'He may come back; I'll leave it, just in case.' Rosina settled the tray on the desk. 'He was probably going to the loo, or something; he seemed in a bit of a rush.'

He wouldn't come back, Anna was certain. She sat down, feeling miserable. On points she had won their little battle, but it was a hollow victory. Keeping a safe distance from him was one thing but rowing with him was another, yet why had he been so nitpicking about those cot-sides, and why had he been in the ward at all...which patient had he come to see? She was still wondering when, a few minutes later, he loomed in her doorway again.

'I left my pen when I was here this morning...on the ward desk, I think... That's what I came for a few minutes ago, then I got a little...deflected.' He didn't smile as he spoke but the aggressive look had gone, Anna noticed with relief, picking up the internal phone and asking May Fenn, who was at the ward desk, to bring out Mr Easter's pen.

'It's a grey Shaeffer with a gold top,' Simon said over her head and she relayed this to May who appeared with the pen, handing it to him with a smile as broad as a toothpaste advertisement, remarking that she could see it was a classy job and didn't belong to one of the nursing staff.

He slipped it into his pocket and as May closed the door, shutting him in with Anna, he looked down at the tea which still sat there, both cups untouched. 'If that's still going perhaps I could stay and drink it,' he said.

'Feel free.' Anna pushed the tray to his side of the desk. The tea was all but cold and he took it down like a draught of beer.

'Sorry about earlier on, snapping your head off like that and being unreasonable. I'd like to apologise. You nurses know the patients best—we surgeons just carve them up.' He didn't ask if he was forgiven or put on the charm. It was a straightforward, *real* apology and,

looking back at him, Anna felt all her defences melting—
felt her insides melting too.

'It's perfectly all right,' she managed to say.

'No hard feelings, then?'

'Absolutely not.' She reached for her tea, lowering
her lids for eyes could be a giveaway. He might see the
relief in hers, and she didn't particularly want him to
know just how glad she was to be back on *reasonable*
terms. . . After all, a girl had her pride.

'The fact of the matter is,' he went on, 'I was in a
tetchy mood. At a little before four o'clock Mrs Gill
rang through to tell me that Miss Benson had gone home
with a bilious attack. Naturally I'm sorry about it, poor
woman, but her absence this evening has put me right
on the spot as I've got three patients due.

'The last thing I want to do is put them off at such
short notice, but it looks as though I shall have to. I can
hardly have them turning up at the house when I've no
chaperon nurse.'

'Oh dear, no, of course not,' Anna sympathised. Her
tea was as tepid as his had been, but she sipped it as
though it was hot. 'I suppose Mrs Gill wouldn't stay
on?' she said, raising her eyes at last.

'She would, if I asked her—' Simon watched her
replace the cup on the tray '—but I can't quite see
her helping me with cultures. . . Two of the patients are
coming for cervical smears. Besides, Mrs G. has a home
to go to and a husband to look after.'

Almost any one of the off-duty staff would offer to
help him out. Rose, from Maternity, would jump at the
chance and so would Jean, or Nurse Cheng. Over my
dead body, Anna thought, hearing herself say, 'I'm not
doing anything special this evening. If you would like
me to help you, I can. I could go home first and freshen
up, then come round, looking the part!' She tried to joke,

to be airy and flip, for supposing he turned her down?

She needn't have worried, however—there was no question of that. Her offer was accepted with such speed that she couldn't help wondering if telling her of his plight had been a means to an end. 'I can't tell you what a load that would be off my mind,' he said, then added, 'To be honest, I wanted to ask you but thought you'd have other plans.'

'None that matter this evening,' she said, just as her telephone rang.

He was getting to his feet as she lifted the receiver and, putting it to her ear, she heard him say, 'See you at six, then,' before he disappeared.

A feeling of excitement fizzed inside her as she drove swiftly home. There was disquiet there, too, which she wouldn't countenance, for going to his home as his locum nurse/receptionist would be a far cry indeed from going as his guest...and drinking coffee...and tripping over his dog. She was going there to work; she would be going in a professional capacity.

Strictly speaking, he ought to pay me, she thought, and smiled to herself, making the driver of the van drawing up beside her at the lights give an appreciative whistle and ask to be let in on the joke.

CHAPTER SEVEN

ONCE back in her flat, Anna changed into a fresh uniform. It would hardly be the thing, she thought, to open the door to Simon's private patients in a creased and work-weary dress. A cap, she felt, wouldn't be necessary, but for absolute neatness she tucked her hair behind her ears where it hung, a silken tassel of colour above the shoulders of her dress.

She had plenty of time; she didn't need to start off for another ten minutes which was why—as she stood by the window, watching Prue oil the front gate—her thoughts strayed back to the evening before, when Alex had brought her home after their theatre date. He'd kissed her goodnight in the car then sat back, facing towards the front again. 'It's a case of "just good friends" so far as you're concerned, Anna...that's so, isn't it?' He still kept staring ahead.

'I'm sorry, Alex... It's not your fault; it's me, I just don't...react.' She was trying so hard to use words that wouldn't make him feel demeaned.

'There's no need to be sorry.' He refastened his seat belt, dipping his head to the task. 'I wish things could be different but, if they can't, there it is. I think that perhaps you're not entirely recovered from your husband's death. Two years isn't all that long to be rid of grief. I've been there myself, remember.' He looked at her again, perhaps waiting for her to confirm that this was the reason why she couldn't come to life in his arms, except in a passive way.

'It's difficult to say,' she dissembled, knowing that

she lied, but she could hardly tell him that she was long over Daniel and that the reason why he, Alex, couldn't strike any spark was that he didn't, and couldn't, attract her—not in a sexual way. 'I'm sorry if you feel you've been wasting your time,' she added, trying to smile.

'I don't feel that. . . Absolutely not!' He looked indignant then. 'I've enjoyed every one of our outings, and I hope you have too.'

'*Very* much!' At least that was true.

'I feel we get on well, and I'd like us to keep on meeting. I'll settle for friendship, if that's what you want, just so long as I know. Contrary to what all the cynics say, Anna, men aren't always just out for one thing!'

'Oh, Alex, what a speech.' She returned his smile, liking him even more. In fact, she liked him a lot, she realised with a little stab of surprise. So she told him that she would like to keep meeting him, but also made up her mind that their outings must be less frequent and the expenses shared.

I don't want him to feel that I'm taking all and giving nothing back, she thought now as, with her mind on Simon and getting to his house, she picked up her shoulder-bag and let herself out of the flat.

He was looking out for her as she turned into his drive. He had the front door open and was coming down the steps before she got out of the car, Buzz at his heels giving short, annoyed yaps as though to say, not *her* again.

His annoyance was clearly not shared by his master, whose sweeping glance took her in from gleaming head to broad-strapped Scholls. 'A sight for sore eyes!' His words made her colour.

'I haven't brought a cap; I hope that's all right?' She swallowed nervously as he ushered her into the hall.

'Not necessary.' He shook his head. 'Even on the

wards it seems to me they're of little value, apart from being decorative.'

'Some hospitals. . .' she followed him up the stairs to his rooms '. . .are already doing away with them—they're a pain to keep on.' She was chattering too much, and knew she was—all this rabbiting on about caps. Even Simon looked rigid about the shoulders. Perhaps he was thinking that it might have been better to put his patients off.

The consulting-rooms looked different bathed in evening light. The fuschia was wilting and dropping its heads, and Miss Benson had plainly left in a hurry for one or two papers lay on the carpeted floor. Simon picked them up.

'When the bell goes,' he said, 'bring the first patient, Mrs Paterson, straight through to me. I usually have a little chat first but you stay within reach, then take her through here to undress—' he opened a door on the right '—give her one of these gowns to put on, then bring her through again, help her onto the couch and cover her up. It's a little like Outpatients' Clinic, Anna.'

'Only posher,' she laughed, beginning to feel a little better in this quiet atmosphere.

'Here are the notes of who's coming.' He laid them on Miss Benson's desk. 'You've just got time to sift through them before Mrs Paterson comes. She's sixty-four, and likes to have an annual pelvic examination, including a smear. You'll find everything you need in here.' He unlocked a small cabinet. 'I use a Sims' speculum and an Ayre's spatula; the slides are at the back and so is the fixative; labels in the desk.

'Miss Turf, who comes next, is a follow-up after removal of an ovarian cyst at the Causeway Clinic six weeks ago. She's a young woman of twenty-five. The cyst was small and I was able to enucleate it, leaving most of her ovary in place.

'Mrs Flower is a new patient so there's nothing much on the notes, apart from her GP referral letter. She's complaining of amenorrhoea, which may or may not be caused after stopping oral contraception. She's forty-two years old. Spontaneous menstruation should return after six months, and she's been off the pill for eight. She may need a course of clomiphene citrate to get her going again.'

'She could be pregnant,' Anna suggested.

'Her GP would have picked that up, I rather think. He's one of the thorough ones; I get several patients from him.'

'Oh, yes.' Feeling slightly foolish, Anna confined herself to reading the notes as Simon went through to the main consulting-room.

A few minutes later she heard the sound of a car turning in at the drive. Quelling one or two butterflies, she got to her feet, hearing Simon call out, 'This looks like Mrs Paterson, missing my gatepost by an inch! Wait till she rings before you go down. She likes to take her time, hates being pounced on. . . She's just a shade difficult.'

That's all I need, Anna thought, but stayed where she was until the sound of the doorbell pealed through the house, making Buzz—safely confined to the kitchen— bark like a maniac. On the doorstep, legs planted wide apart, stood a large perspiring lady in a polka-dotted dress. She was puffing from the exertion of getting out from behind the wheel of her car. She viewed Anna with raised eyebrows.

'You're not the usual girl!'

'No, I'm standing in, just temporarily.' Anna stretched her mouth into a smile.

'I don't like change. . . I like people I know.'

Anna smiled still more, refusing to apologise for her presence.

They went up the stairs very slowly in a cloud of Yves Saint Laurent, which increased in density when, a few minutes later, Mrs Paterson undressed behind the screens.

She was no sooner settled on the couch than she reared up again, fixing Simon with her eye and telling him that during a year something might have gone wrong, so would he be extra thorough as she didn't want to die just yet?

'Have you any reason to suspect there's something wrong?' he asked, as Anna took her gown.

'Well, no,' she admitted, 'no, I haven't, but I like to be sure. My sister died of cancer six years ago and I know it runs in families.'

'There's no medical evidence to support that, Mrs Paterson.' He was gentle and kind, encouraging too, as he positioned her on the couch. 'That's right; that's perfect. Now, try to relax; try to let go. . . Good, that's splendid; won't be a minute now!'

He couldn't have been more encouraging, Anna thought, if Mrs P. had been giving birth. At the end of it all he informed her that so far as he could see there was nothing amiss, apart from natural atrophic changes.

'You mean it's old age?' Mrs Paterson allowed herself to be wrapped in her robe.

'Well, as we get older. . .' Simon began, but was interrupted again.

'I *expect* to degenerate, Mr Easter—' even her expression was withering '—so long as it's nothing untoward, so long as it's nothing worse. Now, I'd like the result of that sample you've taken just as soon as it's back from the labs. . . Get them to give it priority. I don't like hanging about.' She was getting dressed at this point, talking to Simon over the screens.

She was a little less voluble going down the stairs, although she remarked to Anna that getting old was all very well but one had to be *vigilant*.

Miss Turf, who came next, was quieter and easier to deal with. Attractive, slim and young, she answered Simon's questions with confident brevity. . . Yes, she felt well. . . Yes, she'd gone back to work. . . She was grateful for all he'd done.

Mrs Flower, in early middle age, was reassured that once ovulation had been induced by a course of tablets she would begin to menstruate again, and be back to normal. 'You'll realise, of course, that when that happens conception will be possible,' Simon reminded her, scribbling in her notes.

'I do, and I'll get some advice from my GP,' she replied. 'Neither my husband nor I want to add to our family. I had my three sons before I was thirty. We planned things that way.' She looked pleased with herself and just a little smug, Anna thought, watching her swing her feet to the floor and reach for her towelling robe.

She went happily off, remarking to Anna what a wonderful summer it was. She had come in a blue Audi, which she'd left in the shade by the gates. Waiting until she'd driven off before closing the front door, Anna spotted a little brown and white spaniel, bobbing on the back seat.

Inside the house, and confined to the kitchen, Buzz was barking again. 'Shall I let him out?' Anna called up to Simon, who came down at the double, saying he'd do so himself. 'You mean you don't want a chewed-up nurse/receptionist?' She stood back to let him pass.

'Yes, that's what I mean. . . Can't stand the sight of blood!' he grinned, with a return of his old teasing

manner, and Anna rejoiced to see it but hid her pleasure
by staring at the wall. Watch it, she told herself, don't
go dotty just because he's smiled and showed his
charming side.

Buzz elected to stay in the kitchen whilst Simon prepared his meal of meat and biscuit, and set it down for
him. 'I suppose,' he said, going over to the sink to wash
his hands, 'that it would be courting a turndown if I
asked you to stay and share my supper?'

She looked at him, standing there with his back to her
and swishing water over his hands. He had left his jacket
upstairs and his white cotton shirt and dark trousers made
a sharp outline against the window and wall. He was
staring ahead, waiting for her answer, shoulders slightly
raised. The power of his attraction was overwhelming
and she swayed on her feet, hardly recognising—or
believing—her own voice when she told him she ought
to get back.

'Of course.' *His* voice held a tinge of amusement.
'I'm indebted to you for your help.' He seemed to be
wrestling with the taps, then she heard him swear explosively as he swung round to face her. 'The damned hot
water's stopped running—that means the tank in the loft
has run dry! I'll have to go up there. . . Damn it to hell. . .
It's the second time it's occurred!' He brushed past her
and made for the stairs to the second floor, Buzz leaping
ahead and Anna following.

'Have you a proper loft ladder?' she asked.

'No, but there's a folding one in the attics that reached
up all right. I've used it before. Now, you go off home. . .
You don't have to be involved.' He sounded short-
tempered and dismissive, and she didn't blame him at all.

'I'll stay while you're up in the loft. I'd rather.' They
had reached the attics floor.

'Don't tell me you're afraid I'll break my neck!'

'Just a leg, perhaps.' She met his gaze steadily. 'Think what a nuisance that would be.'

'Much though I like your company, I'd rather you stayed at ground level,' he said as they carried the ladder from the attic, and got it hoisted up at the trap.

Anna could see the caverns of the roof space, dark and mysterious. 'I'll stay here,' she promised. 'I don't know much about tanks.'

Simon began to climb, rung by rung, not especially cautiously. He had the look of a man who'd climbed ladders before. He went up, long-legged and lithe, showing a pair of dusty heels and an inch or two of sock. And then he was about to vanish—his head had already gone, one hand was stretched to switch on a light and then the whole of him was illuminated as he doubled up and climbed over the rim of the trap.

Standing there at the foot of the ladder, still leaning hard against it, Anna could hear him walking lightly over her head. The loft must be boarded, she thought, and thank heaven for that—at least he wasn't having to balance on joists and risk coming through with one leg, like people did in films.

But his footsteps had ceased and, straining her ears, she heard a series of thuds, then a hissing, cistern kind of noise which was the water coming into the tank.

'We're in business.' Simon's voice sounded hollow and echo-like. 'It's just as I thought—the ball had adhered to the bottom of the tank. I'll have to get a new one. . . Should have done so before, but kept hoping for the best.'

'Are you all right up there?' Anna called.

'Couldn't be better. . . One thing about the Victorians. . .they knew how to build good roofs.'

The hissing went on for several minutes, and then he came back, filling the trapdoor space once again and descending the ladder, which Anna held on to for dear life—feeling it moving against her hands. It was silly to heave a sigh of relief when he was safely back at her side, but that was exactly what she did—for supposing that ladder had slipped?

'Thanks for staying.' He folded it up and slid it back into the attic.

'I believe in safety first.' Her eyes were on the cobwebby trails in his hair.

'What's the matter,' he asked, 'have I grown two heads?'

'No, just a cobweb or two.'

'Snap,' he grinned, 'so have you—that'll teach you to stand holding ladders for men climbing up into lofts.'

She laughed; so did he, then, suddenly grave, he took her face between his palms. Tilting it up to his, he kissed her, his mouth moving over hers with a sensual, passionate rhythm, flooding her with delight and with a longing for more...much, much more...making every barrier she'd erected between them explode into shivering bits.

When he lifted his head and moved back she felt that she was going to die. 'I'm taking advantage; behaving badly. Good job you're not staying to supper!' He was looking amused; he was *joking*. Oh, how could he, how could he do that? How could he stand there so unaffected when she was still feeling so much?

'It's perfectly all right, but I'd better be going.' She smiled swiftly back at him.

'I'll see you out.' Down the stairs they went, past the consulting-rooms floor and down to the wide, closed front door, where he turned to face her again. 'Thank you for your help, Anna, you did a cracking job.' His hand moved to open the door.

'I enjoyed the change,' she said.

The sun, now low in the sky, made patterns on his

shirt through the coloured panels of the upper door,
reflecting on Anna's face. She could hear him breathing,
or was it herself, or was it the atmosphere sighing
between them? Would he kiss her again. . .? He didn't. . .
He opened the door, and everything changed to sunlight
and glare and formality once more. 'Goodnight, Anna.'

'Night.' She passed him, nearly stepping on his toes;
forced herself to walk sedately over to her car; forced
herself to get inside and switch the engine on.

As she drove off she could see him in her mirror,
moving and going in. She felt regret and relief, with pain
intermixed, and a terrible dragging ache. She mustn't
put herself in the position of being alone with him again.
It's not that I don't trust him, she thought, so much as
I don't trust myself. I could fall in love with him very
easily, but in no way will I get serious with a man who
shies away from personal commitment—who simply
wants an affair of short duration with the kind of woman
who won't care when they part. Almost unbidden, the
striking figure of Julia Trafford sprang into her mind.
Women like her were the sort he needed to offset the
rigours of work.

CHAPTER EIGHT

THE agency nurse who presented herself to Anna on
Wednesday morning was small, blonde and blue-eyed,
with a face like a Barbie doll. Ornamental but useless
was Anna's first thought, but by lunchtime she'd revised
this opinion for Shirley Dobson was a hard worker, deft
and professional. She'd nursed gynae patients before, so
needed little or no supervision, and she got on with
everyone.

Anna knew that Simon was unlikely to put in an
appearance, for he had a full theatre list, including—
from Maternity—two Caesarean sections as Bill was on
leave. Meg did an early round before joining him in
Theatre, but she gave the OK for Mrs Cole to be allowed
out of bed, much to the latter's relief.

'At *last*,' she said, sitting painfully but happily on her
commode, 'and after this I'll walk as far as the desk and
back.' This she did, supported by May Fenn—who told
Anna afterwards that she wasn't quite so chipper on the
return journey; all she had wanted was bed.

Jill Pearson, the perinotomy, was discharged during
afternoon visiting, and a new patient with incontinence
after childbirth was admitted at four o'clock. Anna was
just welcoming her into the ward when Shirley came to
tell her that Mr Easter would like a word with her in the
office. . . 'He's waiting there now and, Sister—' her
blue eyes bulged '—isn't he just *terrif*!'

'Terrif.' Anna's heart gave a jump then, leaving Mrs
Greer in Shirley's care, she made her way swiftly to
the office.

He had his back to her when she went in. He was looking out of the window, which didn't afford much of a view as a thick sea mist was spoiling both the temperature and the outlook, whilst the fog horn on the harbour wall hooted incessantly. Hearing her step, he turned, then came towards her and closed the door.

'Anna, I have to ask this,' he said, without greeting her, 'but did you, when attending to Mrs Paterson last night, happen to notice if she was wearing a sapphire ring?'

The question was so unexpected that she stared at him for a second or two, trying to gather her thoughts. She couldn't even remember, during those seconds, who Mrs Paterson was, then memory swung in and she shook her head. 'No, I don't think so,' she said.

'She rang me last night,' he went on, 'after you'd left; said that her ring was missing, and had I or my nurse seen it when we were clearing up?'

'She was loaded with rings—I didn't notice one in particular,' Anna said, bringing to mind Mrs Paterson's thick, stubby hands. 'And I certainly didn't find one lying around, or I'd have mentioned it at the time.'

'Of course,' he said heavily, staring down at the carpet, 'and, needless to say, I looked everywhere—in the bin where you put the sheets, in the autoclave, all over the floor, down the stairs and out in the drive. She made a fine fuss when I rang her and carefully suggested that she might have been mistaken—might not have had it on. In fact, she was rude to the point of being downright offensive. . .'

'Suggesting, perhaps, that your ''new girl'' might have slipped it in her pocket?' Anna queried with a flash of insight, because, of course, that was exactly and precisely what Mrs Paterson had said—the embarrassed look on Simon's face was telling her that.

And before he could speak—or perhaps because he didn't speak at once—instead of just standing there and looking ill at ease she weighed in with, 'And as you don't know me all that well, perhaps you're wondering that yourself; wondering if I'm to be trusted out of an NHS ward! Well, if that's the. . .'

She got no further for, with one swift movement, he was gripping her arms, fingers biting hard as steel, and half shaking her.

'For God's sake, Anna, I'd trust you with *my life*!' His mouth grazed her face, and for a fraction of a second she felt his lips on her cheek before he released her and went swiftly from the room.

The silence, when he'd gone, was absolute, and within it Anna stood rubbing her arms, and glorying. . .yes, glorying, in his words. He would trust her with his life. . . trust her with his life! It was the ultimate in compliments, and he'd meant it, he'd meant it; he'd left no room for doubt.

Oh, thank you, Mrs Paterson, for being such a cow and trying to blacken my name for if you hadn't he'd never have said what he did—and as for your ring I expect you'll find it somewhere, and even if you don't I simply don't care, except inasmuch as its loss worries Simon, of course.

Next day, Thursday, just before lunch, Miss Benson—having recovered from her gastric disorder—rang Anna on the ward. 'I was told Mr Easter was in Theatre, Sister, and I wondered if, at the first opportunity, you could give him a message from me.' Her voice floated clearly into Anna's ear.

'Of course.' Anna reached for a pad.

'It's not a medical matter; it's about Mrs Paterson's ring. I expect Mr Easter mentioned it to you.'

'That it was lost... Yes, he did.'

'Well, it's found; she found it herself in her soiled linen basket. Apparently, when she got home from her appointment she showered and changed and must have got the ring caught up in something... Anyway, it's found.' Miss Benson sounded slightly scathing and Anna didn't blame her.

'I'm glad for Si- for Mr Easter's sake,' she said, and went on to enquire how Miss Benson was feeling, and was told that she was 'weak but willing and well able to cope'.

Anna laughed, beginning to warm to her—especially when she took the trouble to thank Anna for doing her job the evening before. 'I know everything was a bit of a mess, but I had to leave in a hurry.'

'I enjoyed the change from ward work.'

'You and I ought to meet; perhaps have coffee in the town some time when we're both of us free.'

'I'd like that,' Anna agreed, and knew that she spoke the truth. When Miss Benson suggested the following Saturday week she said yes straight away. They'd have much in common...well, Simon in common, and quite aside from that, it would be good to meet and exchange views with someone completely new.

During the afternoon Anna went down to Theatres with a twenty-one-year-old patient, due for laparotomy. In all probability she would see Simon, she thought, and she could give him Miss Benson's message. Not even to herself would she admit that this was an excuse to run into him. He had been concerned about the missing ring, and she could set his mind at rest.

The theatre suite looked very much the same as all theatre suites. The staff were milling around in various grades and shades of apparel, the nurses in mob-caps, and wearing clogs—the most cool and comfortable footwear when standing for long hours. Anna, walking alongside the trolley, put on overshoes when she passed into the 'clean' area of the anaesthetic room.

'Hello, Mrs Burnham.' John Fell, the anaesthetist, smiled down at the patient. 'Just a little prick in the back of your hand, then the next thing you'll know is waking up in the recovery room and pretty soon after that you'll be back in your own bed in the ward.'

'Good,' she said faintly, too far gone from the pre-med to care very much either way.

Standing behind the anaesthetic nurse and feeling a little 'spare', Anna was hailed by Meg who appeared from the theatre side of the room. 'It's not often we see you down here, Sister.' She smiled behind her mask.

'True.' Anna was about to explain just as, through in the theatre itself, she spotted Simon in a pale blue operating suit—a replica of Meg's—standing with his back to one of the nurses, who was tying the tapes of his mask.

With his fawn hair obscured by his cap, he looked a different person or was it, perhaps, that he seemed different in this closed environment? Behind him, Anna could see the theatre team standing in position, waiting for the patient to be wheeled through. I shouldn't have come, she thought with a flash of panic just as Simon came to the door.

'Nothing wrong, I hope?' When he raised his eyebrows they touched the rim of his cap. There was an aura of impatience about him, and she could hear her voice faltering as she delivered her message which sounded so puerile, even comic, that it was a wonder no one laughed.

'Just as I thought.' Simon's eyes were on John Fell, who was intubating the patient. 'Ready when you are, John,' he said in muffled tones, walking back into the theatre, followed by Meg and two ODOs, one of whom gave Anna a thumbs-up sign.

I should have had more sense than to have come, Anna fumed, flinging off her overshoes in the 'dirty' corridor and going back to the ward. What had she expected, or anticipated—a meaningful look above his mask, grateful thanks for sparing the time to deliver the message herself? I should have left it until he came up to the ward, and if he didn't appear I should have left it to Miss Benson to spread the good tidings when he got home tonight. I made a right pig's ear of the situation, and a bloody fool of myself!

She was off duty next afternoon, Friday, and was shopping in the High Street when she ran slap bang into Alex in the books section of Smith's. Bearing in mind their 'new rule' for meeting, she was surprised when he asked her over to Greystones to tea. 'It's Tom's birthday; he's having a few friends in. You wouldn't, I suppose, like to reinforce the adult contingent—namely, Imogen, Pa and myself?'

'Would I be welcomed. . by Tom, I mean? It's his party, after all.'

'Course. . .he likes you.' Cupping her elbow, as though he felt she might make off, Alex took her over to pay for his book and then they went downstairs in the lift.

On the ground floor she bought Tom a jigsaw. 'I can't crash into his birthday rave and not take him a present. Besides, I like buying for kids,' she said in the face of Alex's protests that a gift wasn't necessary.

'He's invited four boys from his class at school. Oh, and one girl, I think—the female half of an inseparable pair of twins. After tea Pa is taking them all to see *The Lion King*.'

'Your father does well.'

'He's got loads of patience—far more than I,' Alex admitted, as the big car—the Range Rover again—covered the short distance out to West Beldon—and to Greystones, the Marriners' house. Anna had been there once before, when Charles Marinner had asked Prue and her over for drinks one Sunday in July. It was an L-shaped house—its walls partly flint and partly rendered, its roof slate and its windows sash—a perfect family house, Anna thought, preparing to get out as Alex drew up in the drive.

Charles Marriner, sunbrowned and white-haired, his twill trousers hanging slackly on his tall, rangy frame, heaved himself out of a garden chair and came to shake hands with her. 'Good to see you. . . Glad Alex brought you. . . How's your grandmother? Imo and the kids are all down at the paddock.' He waved an arm towards the end of the long garden, which opened onto a field where Tom could be seen riding Greensleeves over a series of jumps.

His audience of small boys and one little girl were standing outside the paling fence, whilst Imogen Rayland called out instructions in her clear, carrying voice. . . 'Lean forward. . . Shift your weight over her neck. . . Keep your hands light. . . Encourage her to stretch her back. That's better. . .much better. . .oh, well *done*!' Everyone clapped as Greensleeves cleared the jump with consummate ease, tucking her heels up behind.

Tom was showing off, which was natural enough, Anna thought, watching him go round the ring again, but as his father called he dismounted at once and, leading Greensleeves, came to the rail. 'Do you like her?' he asked Anna, who was patting the little mare's neck.

She assured him that she did, 'although I don't know very much about horses, Tom.'

'Imo knows everything about them... There's *nothing* she doesn't know!'

'She's like a mother to Tom,' one of the children—the precocious little girl, who was probably quoting *her* mother—told Anna as they went in to tea.

It was laid in the kitchen. A blue checked cloth covered the long pine table, which was all but groaning with the kind of food that children like to eat. There were sausage rolls, and soft white baps filled with ham and cheese; there was ice-cream and jelly, and trifle, and cake, and buns in paper cases. There was a good deal of hearty eating and excited conversation, mostly about the film they were going to see.

Anna, talking mainly to Charles Marriner, was astonished at how Alex was responding to the children—making them squeal with laughter, passing them food, mopping up spillages—becoming, in effect, a family man. Catching her eye at one point, he smiled at her down the length of the table and, although her heart didn't exactly miss a beat, she nevertheless found herself looking at him in rather a different light.

Charles's Volvo estate easily accommodated six children in its rear seats, and they were off and away by half-past five, ready for the performance which started at six. Imogen went down to the paddock to stable Greensleeves, whilst Alex took Anna home. He was going on, after that, to meet a client at Severndean. 'It's a longstanding appointment,' he said, 'and I can't very well put him off.'

'There's no reason why you should—at least not for me,' Anna assured him. 'Anyway, I promised Prue I'd go to the home to see Great-Nan. I go little enough, goodness knows, which, considering I'm in a caring job, is a disgraceful state of affairs!'

It was on the drive home that he told her about the

party he and his father were giving in three weeks' time. 'We're inviting forty or so guests—some of them clients, some of them friends and their husbands, or wives, and partners. We very much hope—' he slowed at the round-about '—that you and Mrs Gatton will come. Selfishly, I'm hoping that you'll come without a partner so that you and I can link up. My stock will go up a hundredfold with you at my side.'

'I think your stock is all right without any help from me.' Anna's mind went back to the afternoon at Mapletons' stand, when Alex had been hailed on all sides. 'But of course I'll come, just with Prue, if you like. I've no one special to bring along,' she added carefully, stamping Simon out of her thoughts.

Her formal invitation came next morning; so did Prue's. 'The Marriners give wonderful parties,' Prue said. 'I went to one the year before last. I think they asked me then because I'd spent a fair bit of money with them, and they hoped I'd keep it up. I suppose I have, to a certain extent, although my little lot must be very small beer to them. As for you, it's plain as can be that Alex wants to show you off.'

'I'm not his to show off, Prue. We settled that the other night, and now—' Anna turned up her fob watch and gasped '—I really must be off.' It was seven a.m. and she was on earlies. Flapping a hand at a perplexed-looking Prue, she bent to draw the bolts of the main front door.

The night report disclosed nothing untoward, and Anna had just distributed the patients' mail when the learner, May Fenn, came into the office to ask why Mrs Dunbavin had had a salpingo-oophorectomy.

'Why did she have to lose both ovaries—she's only twenty-eight, she'll never be able to have a family and she's married and everything?' May had chosen a bad time to ask questions—just before the round—but Anna did her best to explain, with one eye on the time.

'Mrs Dunbavin's main consideration is to stay alive, May. If you'd read her notes, which you obviously haven't, you'd have seen that she has an inoperable tumour of the breast. She has refused chemo or radiation, but having her ovaries removed will dry up her source of oestrogen. Without oestrogen, her tumour isn't likely to spread to other organs.'

'So, she'll be like a menopausal woman.'

'That's exactly what she'll be like.'

'Does she know that?'

'Of course. Mr Easter's explained it to her.'

'Does she mind?'

Anna held onto her patience with an effort. 'I'm quite sure she minded,' she said, 'having a growth in the first place, poor girl.'

'Yes, Sister. . . Sorry, Sister.' Not unduly chastened, May sped off to help Jean with back rubs, leaving Anna feeling guilty at having snapped at her. Teaching was fine when you had the time to do it, but today looked like being one of those days when absolutely nothing went right.

They were very much all right for Mrs Cole, however, for she was being discharged that afternoon and her son was fetching her. 'He won't know me without my bulge, Sister,' she chortled happily. 'I'll be glad when my stitches are out, though. I hope the district nurse won't forget.'

'She won't, Mrs Cole. We've let her know that you are in need of home nursing. She'll know exactly when to take your stitches out,' Anna assured her, going off to speak to Mrs Burnham, whose laparotomy had revealed the presence of a tubal infection which could be treated at home with penicillin, and attendance at Outpatients' Clinic. She, too, was being discharged that afternoon so there would be two beds free, which would be filled almost as soon as the revised list was in Miss Tell's hands.

Simon came to the ward just before lunch to have a brief word with the new patient, Anthea Gordon, who was having a reversal of sterilisation operation. He had learned from her GP that the original sterilisation—carried out in a Leeds hospital five years ago—had been performed by the clips method of blocking the tubes.

Mrs Gordon, who had divorced her first husband, was now married to a man who wanted a child by her... 'Which I want too,' she had told Simon in Outpatients, 'so what can you do for me?'

'I can't *promise* success, Mrs Gordon,' he had told her carefully. 'Much depends on the state of your uterine tubes when the clips are removed, and even if I can restore patency—get them working, in plain terms—I can't guarantee that you'll become pregnant, so it's an "iffy" situation.'

'I'll chance it—I'd like it done,' she had said, and now here she was, sitting up in bed in a strappy nightie, looking glamorous but anxious, too, as she listened carefully all over again to Simon's warnings not to expect too much.

'I hope it's a success,' Anna said when they were back in the office.

'The success rate for that type of microsurgery is around seventy per cent,' he remarked, 'but what I haven't yet warned her is that the risk of tubal pregnancy cannot be ruled out.'

'*Must* you warn her?' Anna regretted the question almost before it was out of her mouth because, of course, he must. It was her right to know.

'I'm not,' he said in a cool voice, 'in the habit of deceiving my patients.'

'No, I know, I'm sorry.'

His head remained bent whilst he wrote in the notes, but he paid attention when she told him that she was moving Mrs Dunbavin to the top of the ward. 'I'm putting her in Mrs Cole's bed—I think she'll be happier there. The thing is that her present bed-neighbour, Mrs Robin, has her daughter in to see her most days. *She* brings her children in, and one of them is a baby in arms.

'Now, I know Mrs D. can't avoid seeing babies for the rest of her life but just at the moment, when she's feeling extra-sensitive, she can well do without having them thrust right under her nose.'

'Good thinking.' Simon looked up briefly, then went on writing.

'It must be awful, at her age, to have to accept the fact that you'll never be able to bear a child,' Anna said, half to herself.

'Some women wouldn't find that too much of a penance.' Simon cursed as his pen ran out. He reached for a ballpoint from Anna's tray, whilst she stared at the top of his head, wishing—unreasonably—that he'd be more conversational and wanting to make him speak. Wanting, too, to provoke and prod him, she said quietly over the desk:

'You say that so glibly. . . You say it as though dealing with women's reproductive organs makes you privy to other things—to what goes on higher up, in their heads and their hearts. Women, even if they don't actually *want* a child, like to know they're capable of having one. Not to be so capable makes them lose their self-esteem.'

He looked up then; looked electrified; looked as though he was about to slap her—or at least slap her down—but all he said was, quite quietly with his eyes

on her face which had flushed carnation-pink, 'I do talk
to women, Anna, and sometimes they tell me what's
in their heads *and* their hearts. I'm privileged in that
respect.'

'Yes,' was the only word she could manage to breathe
out of her mouth.

'So, what's all this about? I thought you and I were
on the same side?'

'Well, yes. . . I mean, we have to be.'

He rose to his feet, still looking at her, and instantly
she was under his spell again. It was like moving towards
him without moving at all; it was like falling into him.

Through the open door came sounds which she heard
as from a great distance—the clashing of bowls in the
sluice opposite, the smothered laugh of a nurse, the
squeaking of rubber wheels in the corridor outside. She
was holding her breath; she was praying, too, that no
one would come bursting in.

He was going to say something important, she was
sure—she could tell it by his stance, by his mouth which,
very slightly open, was showing the tips of his teeth.
She could tell it by his stillness, by his awareness of
her—which had come to the fore again—and she dared
not move so much as an eyelash in case she put him off.

When the door was pushed wider—when Miss Tell
came in—Anna could have screamed for it broke the
moment, which she was quite sure would never come
again. She even fancied that Simon looked relieved as
he moved towards the door, and went out after greeting
Miss Tell, commenting fulsomely on the brilliance of
the morning and how good it made one feel.

Miss Tell had come to ask about the bed state. Well,
of course she had—what else? But to come then. . .to
come then. . . Why couldn't she have waited another ten
minutes, or been tripped up on the stairs? The revised

bed list was handed over, together with the nursing report of the night before, after which Miss Tell did a short ward round, stopping to chat with one or two patients who were being discharged and personally supervising Mrs Dunbavin's move up to the top of the ward.

Mrs Gordon's operation, on Monday, was deemed to be a success. Meg was full of praise for Simon. 'He did a great job,' she said. 'The distal and proximal parts of her tubes were good and healthy. He anastomosed the cut ends, working with a microscope. You should have seen him stitch—he has wonderful fingers.'

'Yes,' Anna said, then added, 'He must have,' and tried to hide her blush by turning towards the cabinet and fiddling with the notes.

CHAPTER NINE

MISS AMY BENSON looked older than her fifty-nine years—being plump and grey-haired and squeezed into a suit too hot for the sweltering morning. She greeted Anna with a tight little smile and eyes that missed nothing at all.

'I felt it would be pleasant to meet,' she said, stirring brown sugar into her cup.

'Yes, I agree.' Anna's hair hid her face as she stowed her shopping under the table, being careful of Amy's feet.

They were in the Primula Café in Ship Street which, although self-service, had cloths on its tables and wheel-back chairs, whilst its customers were the skirted, permed-hair type with supermarket shopping bags.

It was after the matter of Mrs Paterson's ring had been discussed and got out of the way, and after Anna had been thanked all over again for her help the week previously, that Miss Benson, staring hard at her across the round wooden table, made the observation that she looked very young—'to be a ward sister, I mean. I'd expected someone in their thirties, at least.'

'I'm not so very far off thirty,' Anna smiled, aware that in her best blue jeans and white poplin top she looked far younger than she did in her sister's garb. 'I dare say I look older on the job, when my worries are weighing me down!'

'But you like it, do you, and you're settled?'

'I do and I am.' Anna's answer was as direct as the question, and even held some of its sharpness. 'I'm in the speciality of nursing that interests me and I have my own home—a flat in my grandmother's house—so I'm suited all round.'

'How do you get on with Mr Easter?' was the question that came next—one that Anna had been expecting, Simon being their common concern. Even so, she was careful how she answered.

'Oh, all right, I think,' she said, 'but, as you know, consultants aren't very often on the wards—not on a day-to-day basis—so you probably see more of him than I do, working from his home.'

'That's true, of course—' Miss Benson cut her custard tart in two '—and we get on well now that I'm used to working for a younger man. The patients all like him— I wondered if they would, after Mr Duran. He was a very hard act to follow, eminent in his field. Still, it's three years since the change-over and the private list has doubled.'

'Which speaks for itself,' Anna said drily. Miss Benson conceded this, even going on to say that he was a very attractive man. Anna nodded, unable to speak, as some of her poise took flight. Amy Benson didn't seem to notice, however—she was too involved in brushing crumbs off the front of her blouse—and when she next spoke, it was to swerve the talk a little in a very surprising way.

'He operated on my friend at the end of June,' she said. 'Imogen Rayland. You'll remember her, of course. . .had her bladder neck lifted. I visited her once in hospital, but you were off duty, I think.'

'I didn't realise you knew Miss Rayland.' Anna kept her voice level.

'Oh, yes, we met at about the time Mr Duran retired. I started going to evening classes then to take my mind off things. We met there, doing pottery, and afterwards I used to see her riding out at Haverleigh, which is where

I live. I've got a house at the foot of the Downs. She keeps house for the Marriners—lives in—but you'll know that, won't you?'

Anna met Amy's gaze, fully aware that she was being sounded out. Oh, well, so what? She'd nothing to hide. 'I've met her at the house,' she said, 'when I've been with Alex. I like her—she seems very nice, and she was a good patient too.'

'She's got too fond of that little boy,' Amy burst out. 'When Alex Marriner remarries, which he may, she's going to feel usurped. His wife might not want her around, which would mean that her home would be gone as well. Of course she could always come and live with me. I've assured her of that.'

She's fishing, Anna thought, trying to find out how things are between Alex and I. Well, I'm not going to tell her—she's practically a stranger and, even if she were not, it wouldn't be fair on Alex. If Imogen Rayland feels insecure she must take it up with him. So all she said was, 'She shares Tom's passion for horses, doesn't she? I can't honestly see either Alex or his father treating her other than fairly. They all get on so well together— at least, that's the impression I get.'

Miss Benson grunted, but was otherwise silent so perhaps even she could recognise when a door was being firmly closed in her face. She took it in good part, though, and when she next spoke it was to remark that Imogen was sheer poetry on a horse.

'I understand she's been riding all her life,' Anna said, responding thankfully to the welcome change of tack. 'Do you ride?' she asked Amy and was rewarded by a broad grin.

'Lord, no! No self-respecting nag would have me on its back. Since I injured my spine ten years ago I've put on a lot of weight. I go on diets, but never stick to them; I like all the forbidden foods.'

Anna sympathised, and their talk from then on was confined to keeping fit. It wasn't until they were out on the pavement, and preparing to part, that Miss Benson asked if Anna would be going to the Marriners' party. 'It's a fortnight today, as I'm sure you know. . .' She was being waggish again. 'My invitation came yesterday, via Imogen, she can invite a friend the same as everyone else.'

'My grandmother and I will both be going,' Anna told her, fastening her shoulder-bag and looping it into place. The strap dragged on her cotton top, pulling it way from her neck—a very youthful neck—and Amy Benson sighed as she carefully asked:

'And will you be bringing a boyfriend with you?'

'Actually, no, I'll be partnering Alex—that's the arrangement—and I fully expect that Prue, my grandmother, will be joining up with his father. Prue has been to their parties before; she's a valued customer.'

'Should be an interesting evening,' Amy observed, and Anna agreed. She thanked her companion for the coffee, the usual goodbyes were said and then they were going their separate ways—Amy to the car park and Anna to Grants Department Store food hall to get some goodies for Prue.

Being Saturday, it was crowded and people were jostling in the aisles. Making for the queue at the fish counter, where a boater-hatted youth was slapping plaice and salmon and sole and cod cutlets onto the scales, Anna's eye was caught by a man in blue jeans and white open-necked shirt, coming away from the head of the queue, wire basket in hand. *Simon*! Pleasure speared through her as he saw her and came to talk. 'What a place to meet!' she managed to laugh.

'But, then, I'm fond of fish,' he said solemnly, making her laughter more genuine.

'What about Mrs Gill. . .doesn't she do your food shopping for you?'

'Most of it, yes, but I like to keep my hand in, you know.'

She nodded, but the queue was lengthening and he pointed this out to her. 'Better get in it, hadn't you, or you'll be here all day?'

'True,' she said, not wanting to move, not wanting to leave his side, but how ridiculous—how pathetic—to feel this compulsion to stay, especially when he was tactfully prompting her to move away.

Unwillingly she took her position in the queue and he grinned a goodbye and went off in the direction of WINES. Anna sighed and felt bleak.

She was still a long way from the head of the queue when a shrill cry that was all but a scream tore through the hall. It had come. . .was still coming. . .from the third aisle along, which displayed sauces and soups. Shoppers froze in their tracks, turning startled faces in the direction of the noise. Anna acted, and fast.

Rounding the corner and entering the aisle, she ran towards a girl who was lying on the floor, moaning and holding her arm which—grotesquely bent—showed prongs of bone sticking up through the flesh. And at first that was all Anna saw as, feeling herself slipping in a spilled mess that was some sort of oil, she crawled on all fours to reach her.

'It's all right, it's all right, I'm a nurse and I can help you. Please don't try to move or you'll slip again. . . Yes, I know your arm hurts. I'm going to gently support it and keep it out of this mess.'

She managed to do so, the shouts of the girl and the murmurs of the crowd which had gathered round filling her ears. 'Someone get an ambulance!'

'It's been sent for,' she heard, and thank heaven—
thank heaven—there was Simon!

He was kneeling by the girl, asking her name and
soothing her in that special, practised way he had—and
not a moment too soon for, just as Anna was registering
that the girl was hugely pregnant, she shrieked again.

'It's the baby. . . I've started. . . The baby's coming!'
Water gushed between her thighs. She sat blocked
against Simon's legs, Anna fighting to keep her arm still
and hearing Simon telling her, tense-faced, that everything would be all right; that an ambulance was coming
and she'd be at the hospital in a trice.

'My husband,' she cried, 'he's at. . . We live. . .' She
gasped out a number just as the ambulance crew arrived
with their stretcher, and the crowd moved back to let
them through, one irate woman shouting,

'That oil was spilled ten minutes ago. . . Ought to have
been cleaned up. . . Ought to have railed the floor off
till it was safe to use!' The manager and supervisor,
standing by, came in for a beration. Getting up from
the floor as the stretcher was raised, Anna and Simon
followed it out.

'I'm going with her.' Simon climbed into the
ambulance.

There wouldn't, Anna realised, be room for her—not
with the nurse in there as well—so, telling Simon that
she would pick up his shopping and bring it to the
hospital, she re-entered the store, where the manager
asked her if she'd seen the girl fall.

'No, I didn't, but there were a number of people who
must have!' She didn't mean to sound short, but his staff,
and certainly his supervisor, had been shockingly remiss.

'Will she be all right. . .the young woman?' The manager's face was white. He kept wringing his hands and

assuring Anna of irrelevant things like paying for a new pair of jeans—hers were oiled from the knees down. 'We won't charge for your shopping, either, nor for your friend's.'

'My friend,' she told him, 'is a consultant gynaecologist—it was lucky he was here—and I'm a nurse, so that was lucky too!' There was nothing like praising oneself. 'And I haven't done any shopping, but I'll take Mr Easter's and tell him it's a present from the management and that you'll pay for his trousers as well.'

Out in the street again, with Simon's crab and wine in one of the store's plastic bags, she walked to the hospital in her stained jeans and crossed the yard to Cas. Almost before the doors slid back she was hailed by George, one of the ambulance crew, who told her that the girl had given birth in the ambulance. 'She gave a yell enough to wake the dead and the kid shot out, straight into Easter's hands—even he looked taken aback!'

'Is she all right. . .? I mean, with a quick birth like that. . .of course it was the fall. . .?'

'Seemed so; wasn't losing much blood; she's up in Maternity now.'

Over George's epauletted shoulder Anna caught sight of Simon getting out of the lift and made her way towards him, holding out the plastic bag. 'With the compliments of the management. . .crab and wine intact!'

He smiled ruefully, taking the bag. 'Thanks for bringing it.' They sat down on two chairs by the wall. 'The baby's a boy,' he said, 'born in the ambulance—a six-pounder and healthy. Sister Webb's got him in hand. Bill's looking after the girl.'

'How is she?' Anna enquired. Simon was wearing a white coat, most likely, she thought, to cover his shirt. No baby was born without mess.

'So far, so good. She's young and strong, but that arm will take some fixing. She'll need deep anaesthesia, so just as well the baby came first or the poor little devil would have come out fast asleep!'

'She ought to get compensation—she should sue the store. It'll be very difficult for her, trying to look after a young baby with her arm in a plaster—a *long* arm plaster—perhaps for several weeks.'

'You're right, of course...' Simon looked reflective, then he tapped Anna's arm '...but you and I,' he said briskly, 'have done our good deed for the day. It's time we went home. I'll ring for a taxi, assuming, of course, that—like me—you came into town on foot this morning.'

'I did. I like to walk when I can.'

'But not in déshabillé!' he grinned, and looked down at himself, then crossed the department to phone.

They didn't sit close in the taxi, yet there was intimacy of a sort. The little space of seat between them, Anna thought, was no division at all—not when there was this feeling of oneness, of being in total accord. At this moment I know that what I'm feeling he's feeling too. Oh, why can't this ride go on and on, and never ever stop? Yet they *were* stopping, or at any rate slowing, for here was Romsey Road.

'Yes, at The Gables, please; it's marked on the gate,' she heard Simon call out to their driver. Simon's hand came out and covered hers, then he raised it to his lips— an old-fashioned, courtly gesture, which was in no sense an embrace. Yet, once again, it felt like one. His mouth was soft and warm, lingering on her skin for a heart-stopping second and leaving her with just enough breath and strength of mind to say goodbye to him.

*   *   *

Over the weekend their protégée, Gillian Fox, had her arm plated and screwed and encased in a long-arm plaster, but she came through the ordeal well, delighting in her young son and in the presence of her husband who never left her side. Anna saw her briefly on Monday before going on duty, met the baby and was thanked profusely for all she and 'that doctor' had done.

As to the gynae ward situation, it was relatively unchanged, but both Mrs Dunbavin and Mrs Gordon were being discharged that afternoon. Mrs Dunbavin, who had been more relaxed since she was moved to the top of the ward, confessed that she was half dreading going home. 'It's not that I don't want to be with my husband. . .I do, very much. . .but in here I feel protected and safe, just in case things start going wrong.'

'You'll be seen in Outpatients' Clinic and kept a close eye on,' Anna told her. 'Lots of patients feel as you do for, even though you've only been in here a very short time, you've become hospitalised. The world outside seems unnerving—even frightening—but that will soon pass. Why, by this time tomorrow you'll be wondering what on earth you worried about.'

Her husband, a young sandy-haired man—bone-thin with a huge grin—wheeled her out to the lifts at teatime. 'I've missed her a lot,' he said, flushing almost as pink as his shirt as he shook Anna's hand.

Anthea Gordon's husband was older and not so likeable. 'Tell the surgeon that if she's not pregnant by this time next year I'll sue him,' he said. He was joking, but in very bad taste, Anna thought, catching sight of Anthea's strained white face. Had he no sense of timing at *all*?

By lunchtime on Tuesday five new patients had been settled into their beds—two hysterectomies, two prolapses and one fibroidectomy. All underwent surgery on

Tuesday and it was Wednesday before Simon, with Meg in attendance, made his appearance in the ward.

His main concern was for Mrs Chapman, the fibroidectomy patient. He had managed, with consummate skill, to do as she wished and removed her fibroids whilst retaining her uterus. Her blood loss, however, even with the use of a myomectomy clamp, had been alarming, necessitating her being on transfusion for some hours post-op.

'Why she wants to hang onto her uterus at her age is beyond me,' he said. Doris Chapman was fifty and beyond child-bearing age.

'Women are funny that way, sir!' Meg retorted before Anna could speak and say very much the same thing— although not so pertly, perhaps.

It was unusual, she thought, for him to be impatient on the ward, not that a single trace of this showed as he went from bed to bed, saying goodbye to some of the patients who were due for discharge.

He was off on a week's holiday to his parents in Cornwall, starting from five o'clock. Bill Corby would step into his shoes and be glad of the chance, but Simon would be missed. . . . *I* shall miss him and I can't deny it, Anna thought as she watched him pull up a chair by Mrs Chapman's bed, taking time to reassure her that she wouldn't need to go back on transfusion; that her fibroids were all gone; her uterus was repaired and perfectly healthy and very much in place.

'Now, we're going to put you on a high-protein diet— plenty of meat and fish, plus an iron supplement and all the fluid you can drink. This will help continue the good work started off by the transfusion. Once the red part of your blood is up to 10 or 12 g you'll be feeling a great deal better. . .better than you've felt for years.'

'I put you to a lot of trouble, didn't I?' Her nervous

fingers moved over the strip covering the venepuncture wound.

'That's what surgeons are for, Mrs Chapman,' he smiled, and got to his feet, leaving Meg and Anna to follow him to the doors.

'He's due for a break,' Meg said, when he'd gone up to Maternity to liaise with Bill.

'Yes, I know.' Anna nodded, whilst wondering if, after their supermarket adventure, he would come back to say goodbye. He did come back, but brought Bill with him, and they did a short round together. After which it was a simple case of 'Bye, Anna; see you tomorrow week!' with Bill grinning behind his back, sticking his thumbs in the air.

Well, for heaven's sake, what did you expect? Anna asked herself, watching the two of them—one short and one tall—making their way to the lifts. What did you expect him to do—take you for a drink and say that he wished you were going with him? You must be out of your mind. I shall be more settled and calm without him. Bill and I get on all right. A week will soon pass; a week is nothing. How annoying it was that even before he had set off she was wishing him back again.

'It's not so exciting without Mr Easter coming onto the ward,' Shirley Dobson, the agency nurse, remarked later. Jean Ross agreed with her, whilst even little May Fenn said she'd be glad when he came back and mislaid his pen again.

Meanwhile Bill coped manfully with everything that came up. 'He's a grand surgeon,' Meg Brodie declared— she had a soft spot for Bill. 'One day he'll be as skilful as Simon, and he's wonderful with the babies up in the care unit. . . Rose Webb will tell you so.'

The week passed. Patients were discharged; new ones were admitted, and when Simon returned only one of the old ones remained in the ward—Doris Chapman, who had had a slight setback in the shape of a bladder infection for which Bill had prescribed Penbriton.

'If her specimen is clear by the weekend I think we can let her go home,' Simon said, walking ahead of Anna out into the corridor. It was as she made to turn into the office that he swung round and asked how she was.

'Absolutely fine; couldn't be better!' She willed herself not to fill up with pleasure at the simple enquiry. 'And you're looking rested,' she added, moving back to let the voluntary helper with her library trolley go trundling through.

'I had good weather and a load of fresh air,' he smiled down at her, his sun-, and sea-, and wind-bronzed face bracketing into folds. No. . .no man had any right to be so distracting. Anna could feel her whole body tingling as though she was threaded on wires.

She had finished for the day and had already handed over to Jean and the late shift nurses so there was no reason why she shouldn't walk with Simon up the corridor, especially as he seemed to expect her to do so— moving his arm behind her in a wafting movement, like a kind of remote control.

She felt happy; she felt wanted; she felt willing to be under his spell again, for that was the way of spells. They were addictive—she had found that out when he'd been away and she'd wanted him back, if only to smile at her.

What he said, however, as they waited on the landing for the arrival of the lift so took her by surprise that she could only stare at him and gape. 'I understand we're likely to be meeting socially on Saturday night,' he remarked, head uptilted to watch the button lights over the lift.

'Do you mean at Alex's and his father's party?' The

lift seemed to be stuck two floors up—number five button lit, then went out again.

'I'm let out sometimes, Anna.' His smile was the teasing kind.

'Well, of course. . . I didn't mean. . .' Anna's thoughts whirled. Who could he be coming with? Not the glamorous Julia Trafford, for Alex had told her that she was lecturing in Japan.

'I'm escorting Janet Mapleton,' Simon said. 'Her husband—my cousin, Hugh—has a business appointment that night. Jan was keen to go, so asked me to do the honours. I heard through Amy Benson that you and your grandmother will be there.'

'Yes, we will.' Anna was still trying to collect herself. 'I didn't realise,' she managed to smile, 'that you were related to the Mapletons. I met a Mr Clive Mapleton at the Collingham Show. Alex and I went to their stand.'

Simon moved slightly as more people arrived. 'Clive Mapleton is my uncle,' he said. 'My mother's brother. He's the head of the firm and Hugh, his son, is one of the partners. He's involved with one of the roadshows at present—he's in York this weekend. Anyway, that's the arty side of our family—the other's strictly medical!'

Anna wondered if Alex knew of Simon's relationship to the Mapletons. Well, he soon would if he didn't now. How astonishing life was at times. Simon would be there, at the party, and so would she. A little spiral of happiness curled. . .so did her toes in her shoes.

'So, see you on Saturday,' he said as the lift opened before them. It was crowded and, although they managed to get in, they became separated, as well as sardined. When the crowd spilled out at ground level at last Simon waved an arm above the sea of heads and hurried towards Casualty.

*   *   *

'I think I'll buy a new dress for the party after all,' Anna told Prue later that evening as she helped her put her gardening tools away.

'I thought you'd decided on your cream silk.' Prue locked and bolted the shed, wiping her hands on the seat of her trousers as she joined Anna on the path.

'I'd like something with a bit more style and pizzazz.'

'Not, I hope, with a hemline up to your crotch—you'd shock Alex out of his mind.'

'Alex isn't as easily shocked as all that,' Anna said reflectively, 'but have no fear, I'll be reasonably decorous. I just feel like branching out.'

'Well, I'm for my skirt and sequined top that's done duty for two decades,' Prue said, shaking a stone from her sandal. She wasn't a great one for clothes.

Anna found the dress she wanted in a small boutique off the Western Road on Saturday morning. She had seen it in the window. It was of midnight-blue jersey silk with diamanté straps. Its skirt was clinging but wide enough to walk in, reaching to within four inches of shapely knee and making the most of the rest.

'It has style and suits you,' was Prue's verdict as they set off that evening just before eight o'clock. They were later than Anna had wanted to be but Prue had elected to spend more time than usual with her mother at the nursing-home, saying that she hadn't looked at all well and that she didn't like leaving her.

'She's had these upsets before and been all right.' Anna had been less than patient.

'That's easy to say.' Prue was on edge and lacking in party spirit. 'Why the Marriners want to live so far out beats me,' she said, glaring out at the countryside skimming by as though it were an affront.

'They like rural life when they're not at the shop, and

five miles isn't far out,' Anna said, beginning the run down into West Beldon village, at the north end of which Greystones House sprawled behind its matching wall and imposing iron gates.

The sun had set and the opal-streaked sky was lapsing into dusk as she steered carefully into the drive, looking for a space to park—which was hard to find, cars even lining the verge outside. The garden, at first glance, looked full of guests standing about in groups with white-coated waiters sliding between them balancing trays of drinks.

'Let's leave our wraps in the car,' Prue said. 'Save scrumming for them when we leave.' This they did and were crossing the lawn when Alex, who had been looking out for them, met them halfway with his father and Imogen Rayland, who took charge of Prue.

Imogen, Anna saw, looked transformed with her grey hair piled up high, earrings glittering against her cheeks and a pale blue dress of floating material softening her angular shape. Amy Benson, in a white linen suit, waved from the terrace, where she sat with a man like a garden gnome who was smoking a fat cigar.

Greystones was *en fête*. All its ground floor rooms had been given over to the party, whilst the collective sound of so many people laughing and talking was a humming buzz—like a swarm of bees, Anna thought as she stepped inside.

There was background music, but not too much of it; there were flowers everywhere—spiky gladioli, early chrysanthemums, roses in silver bowls. There was a teasing aroma of food and wine and a bar at the end of the hall, whilst the buffet table, running its length, was ideally placed for guests who liked to circulate and go in and out as they pleased.

Anna kept a sharp look-out for Simon as Alex took

her from group to group, introducing her simply as 'a friend of mine, whom I don't think you've met'. It was when they progressed into the garden that she saw him. . .saw Simon by the terrace steps, inclining towards a tiny blonde in a pink dress with a cape.

'There's your consultant over there with Janet Mapleton. Did you know they were related?' Alex asked, steering her in their direction.

'Not until yesterday, no, I didn't.' Anna's eyes were on Simon—on the tall, sharp outline of him against the terrace lights. 'I learned yesterday,' she went on, 'that Clive Mapleton and Simon's mother are brother and sister.'

'It's a small world!'

'Yes,' she managed to say before Simon and the pink girl turned round.

Alex introduced Anna to Janet Mapleton, whose hand-shake was warm. 'Oh, I'm so glad to meet you,' she said. 'My father-in-law told me that Alex had brought a stunning girl to our stand. He didn't realise you were a sister on the ward where Simon has his beds.'

'No, I don't think I mentioned that Anna was in nursing.' Alex rested an arm about her shoulders, as though establishing some kind of claim and making her feel uncomfortable under Simon's silent gaze. More people came up to join them, including Miss Benson and the garden-gnome man, who turned out to be a well-known biographer.

Anna recognised a woman with a bun and glasses whom she'd seen in Alex's shop. She had a military-type man with her, presumably her husband, who started a conversation on Georgian silver and the price it fetched in the States. Under cover of all this and with social skill and smiles second to none, Alex drew her away to be introduced to another group of guests.

There was no doubt that Anna enjoyed herself, but talking to strangers and standing about with a glass in one hand and the other imprisoned in Alex's, was a feat and a strain, and she was glad when they went into the house to eat.

It was ten o'clock and cooler, but still warm enough for doors and windows to be left wide, and several people were eating outside on the terrace or at the tables under the trees. Simon was probably out there, Anna thought as she did a quick scan of the sitting-room where she sat with Alex, Prue and Charles Marriner.

'You've taken everyone by storm tonight,' Alex whispered as he plied her with food.

'I feel as though I've been through one—the eye of it, too,' Anna said edgily, beginning on her plate of salmon and asparagus tips. It was cold and delicious. She was hungry, she realised. After all, she'd not eaten since lunch. Reviving by the second and beginning to feel more well disposed towards Alex's blandishments and to making conversation with other guests who joined them, she winked across at Prue, who was having the time of her life. Her grandmother, she decided, was a social bird, and took parties in her stride.

When one of the caterers came to speak to Alex about opening some more wine, Anna excused herself on the pretext of 'powdering her nose'. The downstairs cloakroom into which Imogen showed her had its sash window raised. So standing there and rinsing her hands she could look out into the darkness of the side vegetable garden, which, she remembered, ran down to the paddock where Tom's little mare had her home.

The wish to be on her own for a little while longer, away from the braying sound of so many people all talking at once, became strong enough not to be resisted and, hitching up her dress, she straddled the sill and jumped down into the earth of a flower-bed below.

She need only be a few minutes but how lovely it was out here, with the noise of the party a background one and in front of her the long path that led down to the paddock, which, now that her eyes had become accustomed to the darkness, she could see quite well. What she didn't see, or hear, or have any awareness of, was the figure in the shadows a few yards behind her—the figure of a man who waited until she was nearly to the paddock before he called her name.

She stiffened and froze. She knew who it was; she knew it was Simon; she didn't need to turn to check this out; she would have known his voice from a dozen others. 'How you startled me!' she cried.

'I was trying not to.' He drew level with her.

'I came out here to be on my own.' She didn't mean that to sound the way it did, as though she was brushing him off.

'So did I.' He fell into step beside her, going on to say, 'As a matter of fact, I was already out when you vaulted over that sill. I was so intrigued by the stealthy manoeuvre that I decided to follow you!'

'Oh!' Reflecting on the figure she must have cut, Anna felt herself blush.

'Perhaps you got bored with your hostessing duties?' They halted at the paddock rail, he resting his arms on the top of it and turning to look at her face.

'I'm not the hostess but simply a guest, the same as you,' she corrected quickly and a little sharply.

'That wasn't the way it looked.'

'Things very often aren't.'

'True,' he conceded, and then a stifling silence fell. Anna's ears sang with the strain of it. What did he want? Why had he followed her? Why was he here?

'He's too old for you,' he said at last, and she heard her own surprised gasp.

'What an odd thing to say!' She peered at him standing there, looking over the paddock.

'By about twenty years,' he went on as though she'd not spoken at all.

'Between friends age doesn't matter.'

He turned round and faced her then. 'You're not trying to tell me that you and Marriner are "just good friends"!'

'That's exactly what we are,' she said with emphasis, glad to put him straight.

She was unprepared for his laugh, which came out like a snort. 'That's not the way *he* feels—showing you off, handing you around like a precious painting, for everyone to admire! The way he behaves, and *the way you let him*, makes me think you're being just a shade economical with the truth!'

It was that that fired her. He thought she was lying. 'You must believe what you like!' she snapped.

'Indeed I must,' he retorted, 'as will most of the guests here tonight. You're a beautiful girl. . .a desirable woman. . .your charms enhanced by that dress! No male with a millilitre of red blood in his veins wouldn't burn at the sight of you!'

'You make me sound like a bimbo!'

'Don't talk such rot. . .don't talk arrant *rubbish*!' He reached out for her, seizing her roughly and jerking her to him, forcing her chin up and bringing his mouth to hers in a kiss that was devoid of tenderness—a kiss that was angry and thrusting, hurting her with its force. And yet. . .and yet she responded to it, just as forcefully— matching anger with anger, passion with passion, stretching her arms round his neck, tangling her fingers in his hair, holding his head down fast.

When he moved back, when his heat was no longer

slammed against her own, when he gave a small trium-
phant laugh, when the cold night air ran like a stream
between them, she told him that she hated him. 'I don't
want to be out of control like that, I don't want an affair!
I don't want sex for kicks, without love. . .and I *don't
want it with you!*'

'Pity!' The single word hung in the air like a bomb
which might explode with the slightest movement from
either of them. 'Better stick to your Ancient Marriner,
then,' he said softly into the night. 'Speaking of whom,
here he comes now.' Following his gaze, Anna could
just make out Alex's narrow, lithe figure moving under
the trees.

She ought to wave, she supposed, or call out, but she
felt too shaken to move and too close to tears so she
simply stood and waited for him to come. He was with
them in seconds, smiling affably but looking mystified.
'I wondered where you'd got to, Anna.' He looked from
her to an imperturbable Simon, who blithely said,

'Blame me, Alex, I kept her talking.'

'And I came out for a breather, which sounds rude
but isn't meant to!' Suddenly glad to see him, Anna
took his outstretched hand, agreeing at once when he
suggested that she might like to say goodnight to one or
two guests who were on the point of leaving for home.

'I should be one of them. I don't want to be late, and
I know Janet doesn't,' Simon put in, walking with them
back up the path to the house.

'You're very quiet,' Prue remarked to Anna when they
were driving home. She, Prue, being the alcohol
abstainer, was in the driving seat.

'Parties exhaust me.'

'They shouldn't at your age.'

'Even so, they do.' Anna folded her arms in her mohair stole, bearing its tickly feel.

'I had a nice chat with Mr Easter and that pretty cousin of his. Fancy them being related!'

Anna nodded wordlessly. She was consumed by thoughts of Simon but in no way did she want to discuss him, and was relieved when Prue went on to talk about Charles Marriner and how much he seemed to have aged.

CHAPTER TEN

HAVING lain awake until four a.m., Anna was deep in sleep when her telephone rang at half-past seven. Stretching out an arm, she croaked a hello into the receiver, blinking sleepily at her clock. Who on earth could be ringing at this hour? It must be an alert at the hospital. The call *was* from the hospital, but it was Alex, telling her that his father had suffered a heart attack.

'Oh, Alex, how awful! How is he now?' Sliding her legs out of bed, she reached for her robe and stiffened herself for the worst possible news.

'He's in Intensive Care,' Alex went on. 'I'm ringing from there. I'm told it was a myocardial infarction, I've been here all night. Imogen and I found him on the bathroom floor when we were clearing up after the party. Anna. . .' his voice altered slightly '. . .could you possibly come? I know it's a lot to ask, but I'd. . .I could do with your company.'

'Alex, of course,' she drew a quick breath '—of course I'll come! I'll be with you in twenty minutes, maybe less!' Putting down the phone, she washed and dressed at lightning speed and bolted down the stairs, startling Prue, who came out of her flat, a mug of tea in her hand.

When she heard the news she shook her head. 'He didn't look well last night—grey, I thought, and sort of strained. I felt he was pushing himself.'

'I'll ring if I can and let you know how he is.' Anna bent down, slipping back the bolts on the main front door and going out into the clear, bright, ordinary morning over to the garage to get her car.

It was only just eight o'clock but, being high summer, the town was already stirring. Car parks were filling up; family parties laden with beach paraphernalia were filing across the road; hotels and guesthouses were opening windows and doors. Anna was reminded of the Sunday she had met Simon down on the beach, nearly two months ago, and had gone home to breakfast with him.

Fancy thinking of that now, though, at a time like this. She filled up with guilt. Yet how could she help thinking about him when he sat in her mind and her heart like a flickering image that would never let her rest? She loved him; she knew that now; she had known it last night— *during* the night when she'd lain awake, hour after thinking hour.

Turning into the hospital yard, she parked in her usual place and was hailed by one of the porters, trundling a bed into Cas. 'Can't you keep away from this place, Sister?' His approving and lustful eye followed her slender pink-jeaned figure as she made for the entrance doors.

An unshaven, hollow-eyed Alex rose from one of the chairs in ICU's waiting-room. 'Bless you for coming!' he cried.

'How is he...what have they told you?' They sat down together.

'They say "stable". I've just been in; he knew me and raised a hand. He's being nursed flat, which surprised me. Surely he ought to be raised up to get his breath better? I realise they must know what they're doing—' Alex gripped Anna's hands '—but it struck me as being so strange, and I didn't feel I could ask.'

'He'll be being nursed flat at present because his blood pressure is low,' Anna explained, trying to reassure him yet be truthful as well. 'After a heart attack blood pressure falls...it's one of the things that happens.'

'He's seventy-three. He could die, couldn't he?' There

was horror, rather than panic, in Alex's voice. He had faced the worst.

'Seventy-three's not old these days, and Charles is basically strong,' Anna told him, wanting to take the fear from his face.

'We've always been close.'

'I know.' She leaned forward and kissed his cheek. 'You go in and see what you think.'

'Alex, I'm not a cardiac nurse and I may not be allowed. . .' she started to say and then, seeing a senior nurse crossing to the outer doors, she made the enquiry and a few minutes later was walking into the big square room where every patient had his own special nurse and where monitors blipped away behind beds, their readings repeated on the screens of a major console at the central nursing station.

The sounds were many and various—the hum of a ventilating machine, the crackling and gurgling from suction equipment, the buzz of strip lighting, the movement of the nurses in their special light uniform and, occasionally, the agitated voice of one of the patients demanding to know where he was.

As Alex had said, Charles was being nursed flat—his long, bony torso naked, apart from a drawsheet placed across his loins. There was a tracheostomy set beside his bed and a defibrillating machine; a drip ran into his right arm and a blood pressure cuff lay nearby. His eyes were closed, his face half-obscured by an oxygen mask. When Anna asked how he was she was told that he was still severely shocked, and was being given blood pressure-raising drugs through the intravenous line.

'How do you think he is?' Alex was pacing the floor when she returned to the waiting-room. 'Did you ask, and what did they say?'

'That there isn't very much change,' she answered

carefully, 'but he's no worse; he's not sliding backwards, and everything possible is being done. Now, look, Alex—' she made him sit down '—why don't you go home and get some sleep, or at any rate rest, then come back this afternoon? I'll stay here till lunchtime and ring if there's any change, but there may not be, not for several hours, and you'll be ill if you go on like this.'

Expecting to have to cajole and persuade him, she was relieved when he said, 'OK, for a few hours, so long as I know you'll be here.'

'I will, I promise. I'll come down with you and ring for a taxi.'

'Yes, I came in the ambulance last night.' He got unsteadily to his feet and followed her out to the lift, bumping tiredly against her. 'You're such a support,' he told her down in the yard, 'and please don't—' he shook his head, deep lines pulling his brows '—tell me that's what friends are for. I'm minus one of my skins this morning, and I can't take painful truths.'

'Oh, Alex!' Alarm sifted through her. . . Don't let him expect too much. . . Don't let him think, begin to think, imagine he's in love with me. . .because I'm not with him. I only wish I were. . .

'This looks like my taxi,' he said more calmly as one of the town's Streamline cars sleeked its way into the yard.

I'm sure I don't need to worry, though, she thought as she waved him off. He's just overwrought, over-emotional this morning, which doesn't surprise me a bit. I care about him but I don't love him, and there's a world of difference between the two feelings. Going back inside, she made her way to the lifts.

She was allowed to see Charles again once the doctors had been. She noticed at once that he was looking more comfortable and was no longer lying flat. 'His blood

pressure's coming up nicely, and his pulse is regular,'
she was told by his nurse, who was checking his drip.
Charles was deeply asleep.

Slipping back into the waiting-room, Anna was surprised to see Imogen Rayland there, trim in the blue suit
she had worn at the show but looking far less composed.
'How is he?' She let go of the door and came fully into
the room.

'Doing very well; all the signs are good.'

'Thank goodness for that; I'd like to see him. . . Any
chance, do you think?' She perched on the edge of
a chair.

'He's sleeping at the moment, but you could ask over
there.' Anna indicated the nursing station, which was
situated slantwise in the corridor to give a full view of
every bed. One of the senior sisters was seated behind
the big curved desk, reading a sheet that looked like a
print-out. Imogen took a good look at her back.

'I shall say,' she said, 'that I'm a relative. . .they won't
know I'm not.' And with that she walked towards the
station, spoke to Sister and, rather to Anna's surprise,
was taken through to see Charles. Well, there was one
thing, she thought, she doesn't lack nerve—telling a fib
to get in. Still, if he's awake he'll be glad to see her,
and quite expect that after four years of close living with
the family she *feels* like a relative.

By Tuesday evening Charles was well enough to be
transferred to the cardiac ward, which made visiting
easier, and Anna slipped in when she could. Either Alex
or Imogen were there every day, sometimes bringing
Tom who, although delighted to see his grandfather, got
restless in the ward.

Seeing him there on Thursday evening when she went
off duty, Anna offered to take him down to the shop for

an ice-cream or a Coke. Half expecting him to turn her down flat, for she still hadn't got Tom's measure, she was pleased when—after a considering silence—he said, 'All right,' and crossed to her side.

The shop was crammed, as it always was at five o'clock in the evening, but with Tom—who had no compunction about pushing—they got through to the counter and presently bore a can of Coke and an iced drink-on-a-stick out to the garden beyond, which was as crowded as the shop.

Anna wasn't all that surprised to see Simon for she knew that he had a habit of buying his evening paper at the shop. Even so, the sight of him standing there with a doctor from Paeds, outlining something in the air with his rolled-up paper, very nearly brought her to a grinding halt and she was glad his back was turned.

The two long plank seats were taken, so she and Tom perforce had to sit down on the parched grass. Anna welcomed this as, with legs all round them, they were hidden from Simon's view—even if he turned round and stopped drawing pictures in the air.

Since the night of the party he had only been up to the ward on two occasions—once to see new patients and once for the teaching round, during which she had disgraced herself by transposing two sets of notes. He had noticed the error at once, and said, 'Toller, not Taylor, please, Sister,' and he'd not made a public fuss.

She'd been grateful, but furious at *having* to be, and furious with herself for letting her attention wander just because he was in the ward. After the round he'd gone off, surrounded by medics, and she hadn't seen him since. Whether or not he knew about Charles, she had no idea, but she supposed he'd have heard through Amy Benson, who would have heard through Imogen.

She couldn't see him now but Tom could for, peering

through legs and passing his tongue carefully over his ice on a stick, he was making a study of who was there, and he soon picked Simon out. 'That man with fawn hair, over there by the wall,' he confided to Anna, 'was at our party on Saturday. He came with Mrs Mapleton before I'd gone to bed.'

'He's a doctor here, or rather a surgeon. His name is Mr Easter,' Anna supplied, shifting a little to let someone get to the shop.

'His feet are moving; he's coming nearer.'

'I expect he's going home.'

'Aren't you going to get up and speak to him?' Tom was already on his feet. He was still hidden by the students in front but, as luck would have it, *they* moved to let Simon pass and his attention was immediately caught by Anna scrambling up from the grass, the little boy at her side. He stopped at once.

'It's Tom, isn't it?' He spoke directly to the child, who nodded unsmiling, plugging his mouth with his ice. 'Looks a good and cooling thing to have on an evening like this. I wouldn't mind having one myself.' And now he was looking at Anna. 'Happy families time, I see!' he said pleasantly enough, but with a quirk to his mouth that she didn't like very much.

'Not as happy as it might be, considering that his grandfather is a patient in Cardiac Care.' She turned round to throw her empty Coke tin into the bin.

'Grandpa's been very ill. Dad slept at the hospital *all night*,' Tom put in.

'I didn't know that. . . When did it happen?' Simon's expression had changed.

'He suffered a myocardial infarction late on Saturday after we'd all gone home. He was in ICU until Tuesday, then transferred to the cardiac ward.' Anna was guarded in what she said, mindful of Tom—leaning against her, all ears, and not missing a thing.

'Dad's with Grandpa now, and when he comes down we're going to the Sea Life Centre,' he piped up, wiping a sticky hand down the front of his jeans.

'Sounds fun.' Simon's expression was still hard to read.

'There'll be seahorses there.' Tom's tongue was loosened.

'But not the sort you can ride.'

'Course not,' came scathingly, then, 'Here's Daddy now!' Off Tom went like a speeding rocket, as Alex's immaculate, questing figure appeared in the door of the shop.

'I wouldn't,' Simon said in the few seconds Anna and he had to themselves, 'have made such a fatuous comment if I'd known Charles was ill.'

He meant the quip about happy families, Anna realised, and gave a little shrug. 'What amazes me,' she said, 'is that you *didn't* know. I would have thought Imogen would have told Amy Benson, who would have passed the info to you.'

'Amy is in Wales on holiday this week, staying with her mother. She departed the morning after the party.'

'Oh, well, that explains it, then.'

'I suppose *you* didn't think to tell me?'

'Oh, I did, several times,' she said, 'but it wasn't all that easy to buttonhole you this week, so in the end I gave up.'

'You mean I gave you no chance?' One eyebrow rose.

'Let's just say that I felt it best not to raise any personal issues. Anyway, I assumed that you'd heard. . .' was all Anna had time to say before Alex and Tom reached them, when the matter of Charles's progress was briefly discussed before Simon took his leave.

'He seems a caring type,' Alex remarked as they walked down to the sea front.

'He should be—he's in a caring profession,' Anna said, so briskly, and with such a snap to her voice, that he glanced at her in surprise.

There were five admissions to the ward next day, one of them a Spanish girl—a young language student— who was admitted from Casualty after miscarrying a fourteen-weeks foetus. The mother of the family with whom she was billeted had brought her in, but had since left in obvious relief, and who could possibly blame her? Anna thought, glad to find that Maria could speak English reasonably well.

'Please, have I lost the baby?' She pronounced each word with care.

'Yes,' Anna told her, not knowing whether she was conveying good news or bad.

The big, dark eyes searched her face. 'Then why do I need to be here?'

'Because you need a small operation, Maria, to make quite sure there is nothing left behind in your womb that might cause trouble later on.'

'Will I have it today?'

'Yes, just before lunch.'

And now her eyes swam with tears. 'My friends go back to Bilbao this morning. My boyfriend, José, too.'

'You'll have your operation, which we call a D and C, at twelve o'clock today, but you certainly won't be fit to travel. You'll be sleeping all afternoon.'

Maria wept in earnest and Anna drew the curtains round her bed, sending May Fenn to comfort her, the two being about the same age.

'What the hell was she doing coming to England three months gone?' Meg said irritably. 'Surely the Spanish medicos couldn't have missed a thing like that.'

'They might have if she didn't mention it. She wanted, she said, to come over here with her boyfriend. She didn't expect to abort. In fact, she said, they both wanted the child and would marry as soon as they could.'

'Love's young bloody dream!' Meg said explosively, yet none of her irritation showed when she went to talk to the girl. 'She's on Bill's list,' she told Anna. 'Simon's got a section at midday—twins, and one of them's breached. You ought to go and watch.'

'Can't spare the time, and I don't think he'd want me taking up students' space.'

'You're not like Sister Hilton, are you?' Meg clipped her pen to her coat. 'She'd have been there *and* well to the front. She was one of his ardent fans.'

'Yes, well, we're all different, aren't we?' Anna stopped to help one of the second-day post-op patients get a book out of her locker. Thelma Cannon, who'd undergone a hysterectomy, had come in with her left arm in plaster, having fallen three weeks previously whilst exercising her dog. 'Nothing like coming in plastered!' she'd joked. She was a big, jolly, overweight woman, who bred Pekinese.

Maria Lomez had her D and C at midday and was back in the ward by one. Already coming round, she was laid on her side and told there was nothing to worry about. She was fully conscious by half-past four when Simon came into the ward. There were still one or two visitors around, and at Maria's bedside her boyfriend, José—a flamboyant young Spaniard. The two of them sat clasping hands.

'Draw the curtains round and he'll be in there with her!' one of the patients told Simon, with her eye on the young couple. 'You know what they say about Latin blood!'

'I don't suppose it's a great deal different from the English variety, Mrs Kerr. And what is more,' he added for Anna's ears alone, 'she won't be fit to travel back to Spain tomorrow. She can be discharged to her host family, who I understand are concerned about her, but she would be unwise to make any long journeys until after the weekend.'

'I'll make sure she's told that.' Anna accompanied him to the ward doors. The last of the visitors trickled out, and she was watching the lanky figure of the desolate José walking up the corridor when Simon told her that he was going to see Charles Marriner before he went home.

'He'll be pleased to see you,' she said a little stiffly. 'He's doing really well now. Alex tells me he might be discharged next week when he'll convalesce at home, taking it really easy—but Miss Rayland will see to that.'

'Seems to me she's the linchpin of that establishment,' Simon said, walking away.

Back in the office, Anna wondered how he'd managed without *his* linchpin all week—namely the redoubtable Amy Benson, who was holidaying in Wales. He hadn't asked her, Anna, to help him; hadn't so much as mentioned Amy's absence until yesterday outside the hospital shop.

It was possible, more than possible, however, that the reason for his silence stemmed from the fact that in no way did he want any help from her, not after Saturday night. . .when she'd told him she hated him.

On Monday the news filtered through, via Meg, that Amy Benson was up in Parker Ward, having been admitted as an emergency with acute abdominal pain late on Saturday night.

'Good Lord, what was the matter with her?' Anna

dumped a pile of notes on the ward desk and gave her whole attention to Meg.

'Inflamed appendix, about to perforate. Anyway, it's out. Dan Mansell operated, and this morning she's up and walking about the ward, according to Simon.'

'Poor Miss Benson. I'm sorry to hear it.' But how would he manage with no secretary/nurse for at least another fortnight? Anna's thoughts ran amok.

'She'd just got back from Wales, apparently. . . Staggered off the train at Charding Station, and they called an ambulance.'

'Poor Miss Benson,' Anna intoned for the second time, then for the third—rather more concernedly—when Simon came onto the ward.

'Yes, it's shaken her up.' Simon was signing scripts, sitting in a bar of sunlight that striped across his back. His hair lay pelt-thick, tapering down to his nape, where it moved on his collar, and she longed to touch it. It was all she could do to control her hands and keep them at her sides. 'Still,' he looked up, and she started guiltily, moving back as he said, 'that inflamed appendix would account for her gastric attacks.'

'Almost certainly, yes. . . She'll be far better now.'

'In the meantime, of course, I'm going to miss her.'

'How will you manage?' Anna dared to enquire. But she mustn't offer to help, must she, for that would be lunacy?

He was looking at her steadily, holding her eyes with his as he unrolled himself from the desk and stood up, leaning against its edge. 'I employed a nurse from the agency when Amy was in Wales,' he said, 'and I was lucky enough—this morning, when I rang—to get the same girl back for as long as I need her. She seemed very willing to come.'

I bet she did. 'Oh, so you're fixed!' Anna forced a smile to her face.

'In that sense, yes.' He didn't smile back but, from the way he spoke, she felt that he was only too well aware that it had been on the tip of her tongue to offer her services once again, and this was confirmed when he added, turning away and making for the door, 'You mustn't concern yourself with my troubles, Anna. I can usually sort myself out.'

It's called the brush-off, she thought after he'd gone; he wants nothing more from me. And once again she had that feeling of a door being closed in her face.

'Trouble always comes in threes,' Amy Benson declared next morning when Anna paid her a visit in Parker Ward. 'Mr Marriner was the first casualty, wasn't he, and now there's me? There's bound to be another one—better keep your fingers crossed.'

Anna smiled but said nothing, her main concern at that moment being of the passing of time. She was on the late shift and in another ten minutes was due on her ward.

'You look older in uniform. I'd hardly have known you,' Amy went on, her lacklustre eyes taking in Anna's hand-span waist, shown to advantage in the dark purple dress with its silver-buckled belt. 'But it suits you,' she added more generously, 'and thanks for the magazine.'

'If there's anything else you want, give me a ring at home.' Anna was about to write down her number when Amy informed her that she was being discharged that afternoon.

'My mother's coming for me, and she'll look after me at home. She came all the way from Rhyl when she heard what had happened to me. She's over eighty, but she'll help me cope over the next week or two.'

Anna, who was having difficulty imagining Amy with a mother, said how glad she was that she'd have help at home. 'You only had the operation on Saturday and you're bound to feel odd at first.'

'An uncomplicated appendectomy is nothing these days,' Amy said, sitting up straight—no doubt to prove her point. 'In some hospitals it's done on a day basis, even with someone as old as me, but, of course, you'll know that, won't you?' she added, then exclaimed in the same breath, 'Why, here's Mr Easter. . .now, aren't I a lucky girl!'

He had brought her fruit, three perfect peaches in a little Cellophane box. He laid them carefully on the bed and made to fetch a chair but Anna, getting to her feet, gave him hers. 'I was going anyway,' she said, keeping her eyes on Amy and not him as she spoke. 'Bye, Amy, get well soon.'

'I will, and thanks for coming,' she smiled, but her attention, now, was all on Simon, who was waiting until Anna had gone before sitting down.

No one could fault him on manners, she thought, casting a sneaky eye over her shoulder as she passed through the ward doors. He and Amy were chatting together and, being the nice man he was, he wouldn't be forgetting to tell her how much he was missing her, and how much he was looking forward to having her back.

Amy would love that. She would preen herself, and who wouldn't, for goodness' sake? She would also, with her prophetic tendency—which inclined towards morbidness—no doubt tell him that with the habit troubles had of never coming singly and that, bearing in mind that there were two casualties already, there was bound to be a third.

She was right, too. There was a third, for when Anna got home at a little after ten o'clock that night it was to find her grandmother waiting for her, looking shaken and distraught, with the news that Great-Nan had suffered a stroke and had died an hour ago.

CHAPTER ELEVEN

ANNA'S parents—Diane and Paul Gatton—drove down from Reading next day. Anna was on late duty again, so was able to see them before setting off. In fact, her car and theirs met nose-to-nose at the gate. She drew to the side to let them in and then got out to greet them, whilst Prue came running down the steps to be hugged and kissed by her son.

'I wish I could stay, but I can't.' Anna drew away from her mother.

'See you tonight.' Diana Gatton watched her get back into her car.

'Around ten, yes,' Anna said, then, before slamming the door, asked her mother to be careful of what she said to Prue. 'Don't go telling her it's all for the best, or anything like that. She knows it is, but she doesn't want it said—at least not this morning.' Her mother, she knew, wasn't renowned for her tact, and she didn't want Prue upset.

'I'll watch every word.' Quite unoffended, Diane waved her off—a tall slender figure in a grey and white shirt-waister dress. Anna took after her in looks, but favoured her father in temperament—a big man with a big heart that often ruled his head.

The previous night she had moved down with her grandmother, not liking to leave her alone. She had slept, too—out of sheer weariness—but suspected that Prue had not. Poor love, she must be feeling weird, she thought, for situations like this were many-sided and complicated as well.

Great-Nan had had more than her fair share of life and it was high time she went but, having said that, she'd been Prue's mother. One couldn't discount that fact, which was why Prue couldn't raise a smile this morning and why she felt physically sick.

'And as to how *I* feel,' Anna muttered, pulling out to pass a van, 'I suppose not a lot, to be honest, but then I hardly knew Great-Nan. If I feel anything it's guilt for not having visited her more. It's Prue I feel for, and I hate seeing her sad.'

Having to go on duty, however, and having to immerse herself in the problems of ward management was a respite of sorts, as all thoughts not connected with the patients had to be laid on one side.

The ward lunches were just finishing and then came the quiet hour, when Jean informed her that Simon would be coming up at four o'clock to meet Emily Bagley's husband, who was pressing for his wife to have keyhole surgery.

'She's not suitable for it because of her weight. She was told that very definitely, in Outpatients,' Anna replied.

'Yes, well, Mr Bagley needs to be convinced. He rang up this morning, and contacted ''Sir'', who promised to see him,' Jean said, pushing Emily's notes nearer to Anna's hand.

Looking through the viewing window, both Anna and Jean could see Emily Bagley sitting on her bed and combing her hair, which was the long, thin straggly kind, just beginning to go grey. It wasn't surprising that she didn't want to add to her family as she was forty-six years old. She had five children all under ten, had come off the pill and had opted for sterilisation—which would simplify things, she'd said.

She had been perfectly happy with the advice Simon

had given her as to the method of approach. Now it appeared that her husband didn't like the idea of a long, stitched wound.

'She's not just fat, she's obese,' Anna said, turning round to Jean again.

Once the report was finished she did her round of the ward, placating one patient, Mrs Strong, who didn't like being catheterised. Another patient complained that her bell wasn't working and another about her lunch, which was 'fish again, and boiled, and disgusting' and giving her terrible wind.

Going into the ward kitchen with a dirty cup, which she had found in the ward, she found Rosina nursing a bloodied leg. 'I caught it on the bin when I fell just now, Sister. . . There's not much skin on shins.'

'No, Rosina, quite right.' Anna bent to examine it and found the damage sustained not much more than a graze. It looked much worse than it was. Little Nurse Cheng applied a dressing, after which Rosina limped about with a martyred expression but flatly refused to rest. Anna was filling in an accident form when the visitors began to arrive, rustling bags and bunches of flowers and complaining about the heat.

Just before four o'clock Mr Bagley made his appearance—a wiry little man with a neat moustache and a smiling, affable manner. 'It's not that I want to be obstructive, Sister, in any way at all, but I don't want Emily to be traumatised or in a lot of pain afterwards.'

It was at this point exactly that Simon put his head round the door, whereupon he and Mr Bagley repaired to the interview room, leaving Anna to get on with her work and Mrs Bagley—all unsuspecting in the ward—to forage in her locker for fruit.

Roughly fifteen minutes later Mr Bagley sailed in to join her, putting his arms round her ample shoulders and kissing her on both cheeks. Simon came back to Anna with the notes. 'Is all well?' she asked, gleaning nothing from his expression. He looked hot and tired, she thought.

'Well, he's reconciled now, if not deliriously happy— but there it is. There's no way I'm going to chance laparoscopy on a patient who is carrying at least twenty-eight kilograms of excess weight.'

'She should diet,' Anna said to his back, for he was looking through the viewing window.

'Get the dietician down to see her—couldn't do any harm. Oh, by the way—' he swung round and faced her '—I've just run into Alex Marriner on his way up to Cardiac to fetch his father home, but you'll know about that, I dare say. . .'

'Oh, Lord, I did!' Anna's eyes flew wide. 'Oh, how could I have forgotten? Alex rang last night to tell me, and I said I'd see Charles before he left!'

'You could still make it, couldn't you?' Simon suggested offhandedly.

'No, I've missed my chance. I'll have to leave it. It'll make too much of a flap if I go up now. I meant to come in earlier and see him just before lunch. The thing is, I'm not really concentrating well. My great-grandmother died yesterday.'

'Did she now?' His expression changed, and he retraced his steps from the door. 'How's Mrs Gatton taking it?' He sat down in the visitor's chair.

'She was fantastic last night when she got back from the nursing-home, but a bit low this morning.'

'Should you be here. . .? You could have got leave, you know.'

'I suggested that, but she wouldn't hear of it.' Anna pushed herself, and her chair, clear of the desk but still sat there in case he thought she was trying to hurry him off, which was the last thing she wanted. 'My parents are with her now,' she explained. 'They arrived just as I came out.'

'From Reading?'

'Yes. Dad is her son, but I think I told you that.'

'You did,' he affirmed, glancing towards the door as Rosina appeared with a glass of squash for Anna. It was too hot for drinking tea. He asked her what she'd done to her leg but refused her offer of squash, waiting patiently for her to go out again, which, after a sigh, she did.

'Was Mrs Gatton with her mother when she died?' he asked once the door was closed.

'Yes, she was.' Anna sipped her drink. 'They were having tea out in the gardens. . .Riverside has lovely grounds. Great-Nan was in a wheelchair, thoroughly enjoying it all, when she gave a sort of cry, Prue said, and rolled forward onto the grass. Prue thought she'd arrested at first, but it was a stroke. . .a CVA. . . She lapsed into a coma and died three hours later with Prue at her side.'

'Well, at least it was relatively quick and she'd have known nothing about it,' Simon said, gently and sensibly, 'and in time Mrs Gatton will be glad she was there, right on the spot, shocked though she must have been.'

'She's glad now. It comforts her to know exactly how the end came.'

'Your grandmother is a remarkable lady.'

'The mostest,' Anna agreed, warming to his words and smiling at him, getting the kind of smile back that surely wiped out any ill feeling which might have been rumbling around since the night of the party when she'd told him she hated him.

'Let me know if I can help at all,' he said, and she told him she would. Then he got up to go and, desperate to keep him for a few minutes longer, she asked him how Amy Benson was. 'I know, of course, that she's gone home.'

'Went last night,' he said. 'Far too soon, in my opinion, but there you are—that's the way things are these days and we can't change the system. Her mother, a formidable lady in her eighties, is looking after her with the aid of the district nurses, so she'll have all the care she needs. I'll be ringing her up from time to time to see how she is.

'The agency nurse I've got is first rate but, rather to my surprise, I'm missing Amy's bossy presence, even her annoying habit of treating me like a new boy just out of medical school!'

'I'm sure she's anxious to get back,' Anna laughed.

'All in good time. Now, remember me to your grandmother, won't you?' He opened the door to admit Meg, who had come to tell him that he was wanted in Theatre Two.

When Anna got home that night, just before ten o'clock, her parents and Prue were ticking off items on a long list of things to do. The funeral was fixed for midday on Friday, which didn't give them much time. 'But we were offered that slot and didn't want to miss it,' Paul Gatton explained in a quick aside to Anna when Prue was out of the room.

About ten relatives and friends had been notified and eight were coming, travelling, as it happened, from easy distances and so wouldn't need putting up.

'We're taking them to the Ambassador for a slap-up lunch afterwards,' Prue explained, 'making it as happy an occasion as possible, and then on the Saturday, Anna, I'm going back to Reading with Paul and Diane—just for a few days.'

'We aim to hold on to her for a week at least,' Paul

Gatton said, bending down to his mother and planting a kiss on her cheek.

'You won't mind me not being here, will you, dear?' Prue was looking at Anna.

'I'll miss you and I'll be glad to see you back, but you need a little break. I'll see to the garden and everything.'

'Anna—' her mother put in, setting down her night-time glass of whisky and ginger '—doesn't mind being on her own. She got used to it when she was married, with Danny so often away.'

No one said anything but Paul Gatton's face tightened, whilst Prue looked askance at the daughter-in-law of whom she was fond but deplored her clumsiness.

Once upstairs in her flat Anna telephoned Alex to say how sorry she was not to have seen his father before he left the hospital. 'I truly meant to do so,' she said, 'but this business of Great-Nan threw me and, what with Mother and Daddy coming and everything, it completely slipped my mind. Tell me, how is he. . .how does he seem now he's home?'

'Tired, but we're keeping him in bed for a week on the advice of our GP. It's great to have him back, Anna, you've no idea.'

'It was a very anxious time.'

'You were such a support. . .' There was a little pause, then Alex asked how her grandmother was.

'With Mother and Daddy here, much better. Now it's she who needs support.'

'Perhaps I could come over and see her tomorrow, in the evening, if you'll be there?'

'I will be—I'm on earlies tomorrow—but can you leave Charles?' she asked.

'Easily, yes. Imo will be with him,' he assured her swiftly. 'She doesn't mind what she does in the nursing line, which frees me to go to the shop and keep the business ticking over.'

Looks like Simon was right, Anna thought when she put down the phone. Imogen Rayland clearly holds that family together. I can't see her leaving it to live with Amy Benson, she's far too deeply entrenched.

On early duty next day, Anna was up and out of the house by seven o'clock, seen only by her father who was coming in from a stroll in the orchard—a big, broad-shouldered man in jeans and an open-necked shirt. Bending almost double to do so, he put his head inside the car. 'I've hardly seen you, darling!'

'I know—' Anna looked rueful '—but I'll be home by five tonight.'

'How about me riding along with you now, as far as the hospital? The walk back along the sea-front will do me good.'

'Brilliant!' Anna leaned sideways to unlock the passenger door. 'But it's a good mile back, Dad... Think you can manage it?'

'Cheeky monkey, and me in my prime!' He slid into the car, settling the seat belt over his chest and bending the sun-flap down. 'I want to know how things are going for you,' he said as the little car slid down the drive into Romsey Road and turned towards the sea-front. 'I know you sound happy enough in your letters and over the phone, but now you can tell me to my face exactly how things are.'

'I've left the past behind, Dad, and I'm getting on with my life,' Anna said steadily, tailing a long pantechnicon bound for the port. 'I love my job—the responsibility of it—knowing that I can cope. I wouldn't want to go back to staffing. I quite fancy myself as the boss!'

'How do you spend your spare time?'

'Oh, in all sorts of ways. I've joined the hospital recreational club, although I've not been as yet. There's always the lure of the beach in summer and there's Prue's garden too, which takes some keeping in order and I enjoy helping with that. I do go out on dates occasionally, but I don't want to get too heavily involved just yet. I need a little space.'

'What about work colleagues?'

'Absolutely fine. The nurses co-operate, I've got a very good staff nurse, who's a friend as well, and the surgical team are fine.'

'Your grandmother tells me you have a charming consultant.'

'I think,' Anna said, putting her foot down hard to avoid a jogger on the crossing, 'that Prue's fallen for him, hook, line and sinker, and she a hardened case... All because he admired her clematis! There's no doubt about it—the way to Prue's heart is through her climbing plants!' It was necessary to joke to hide her feelings, which she felt must show on her face. Why, even the sound of the word 'consultant' made her tense these days.

There was a little more talk about Prue, and the way she had taken her mother's death. 'I'm glad she's going back with you after the funeral. It'll be just the break she needs.'

'Hope so,' her father said. 'She can help me in the clinic, if she likes. Once a vet always a vet... seventy-plus or no.'

They were nearing the hospital complex, and Anna turned up the slope, driving slowly past Outpatients and the Tower Block to the main building with its porter's lodge. 'This is where I tip you, darling.' As she pulled into the side, a cream BMW passed them and drew to a halt further on.

It was Simon and he'd seen them—Anna knew he

had, for he'd glanced at the car as he passed. He was getting out. She could see his legs, then the whole of him as he stood up, turned round and came towards them, shading his eyes from the sun. 'Daddy, this is Simon,' she just had time to hiss at her father before he reached them and then she was fumbling to get out to introduce the two men. Her father, already out on the pavement, was looking with interest at the personable man in his mid-thirties, now at Anna's side.

'Simon, this is my father,' she said. 'Daddy, this is Mr Easter, our gynae consultant.'

They shook hands, each taking a keen look at the other. Then they chatted for a minute or two, Simon referring to Great-Nan's death and Paul Gatton saying that she'd been a game old girl. As for Anna, she stood and looked at the two of them, standing there in the sun.

Comparisons, as she well knew, were odious, but she made them just the same, noting how both were the same height, one casually garbed and one sleekly suited as befitted his job, one dark and the other fair, but both. . . and her heart gave a little lurch. . .both of them lovable.

They were laughing now, and Simon was saying, 'I understand your patients are the four-legged type, sir!'

'In the main, yes,' her father replied, 'although I have the two-legged, beaked sort occasionally. In my business, Simon, it's the owners who give the most trouble.'

'Now that I can believe,' Simon laughed, and shortly after that he and Anna got into their cars and goodbyes were said. Paul Gatton started his walk down Ship Street to the sea-front, whilst Anna followed Simon onto the parking lot, where he caught up with her again.

'I still think you should have had some compassionate leave,' he said, as they walked side by side to the hospital entrance. 'You could have had more time with your folks.'

'I've got tomorrow—the day of the funeral—off and it's my weekend off, too, so it's not bad, and I'll see so many relatives tomorrow it'll keep me going for years,' she said offhandedly, still shaken to the core by the wash of emotion she'd experienced when she'd seen Simon and her father shake hands.

Once on the ward, though, there was no time to reflect on anything other than jobs to be tackled, patients to be calmed and breakfasts to be served—cereal, or toast, marmalade or jam, eggs, if supplied from home, usually boiled bullet hard for Rosina lost count of time.

For Emily Bagley there was nothing as she was due in theatre at nine. Anna checked her prepping, fixing her identity bracelet on. 'You'll be back with us in no time, Mrs Bagley.' Woozy from the pre-med, Emily smiled and rolled her head as the porters slotted their poles into her canvas, lifted her onto the long narrow trolley and then wheeled her out of the ward.

After Emily a young woman for repair surgery went down, followed by another with tubal blockage, followed by three D and Cs and a hysterectomy. Both theatres were in use, Simon in one and Bill in the other, with Meg assisting Bill. So it was all coming and going—all ducking and diving, as May Fenn, the learner, said. Still spry and eager to learn as ever, she cheerfully supported the heads of vomiting returnees, and comforted them as well.

Anna, on her way to the canteen at lunchtime with Rose Webb from Maternity, caught sight of Simon in the corridor leading to the doctors' dining-room. He turned and waved, then hurried on.

'He fancies you,' Rose said. 'It's those gorgeous boobs of yours, not to mention. . .'

'He's like that with everyone.' Anna went pink, to Rose's further amusement.

'Indeed he isn't; he's usually pretty tightly buttoned,' she said. 'He doesn't flaunt his charms, or at least he doesn't within these walls. What he does outside them, of course, is anybody's guess!'

'And no one's business,' Anna said tartly, causing Rose, with a glance at her, to change the subject and ask how Alex was.

He was already there when she got home that evening, having tea with her parents and Prue in the sitting-room that overlooked the back garden. They all looked up as she entered. 'Oh, Anna, there you are!' Prue exclaimed, moving to refill the teapot, which Anna took from her grasp.

'I'll do that. . .boil some more water.' She smiled round at them all. 'So this is what you do in my absence—sit around guzzling tea!'

'As you do, on the ward, I'll be bound!' her father teased, whilst Alex, in all seriousness, said that he doubted it.

'On the two occasions I've seen Anna in action, she was working harder than her nurses.'

'I can believe that,' her mother remarked, just as seriously. 'I wish the uniform wasn't purple, though, it doesn't go with her hair.'

Prue refuted this with heat and so did Anna's father, Alex carefully agreeing that purple was a difficult colour to wear, but adding that Anna, with her clear skin, could get away with it.

Thereby offending no one, Anna thought, staring at herself in the kitchen mirror as she waited for the kettle to boil. Alex—a peace-loving man—would be easy to live with for he'd never allow himself to quarrel, let alone have a blazing row.

CHAPTER TWELVE

INSOFAR as any funeral can be said to have gone off well, Great-Nan's did exactly that. The hotel luncheon afterwards, which had been Prue's idea, gave relatives and friends a chance to unwind in a cheerful atmosphere. Back at the house for tea and more talking, the day had begun to drag, but when the very last guest had driven away or been taxied to a train Prue was still game for an evening walk along the front with her son.

'She's got more energy at seventy-plus than I have at fifty,' Diane Gatton, with her feet up, remarked to Anna when they were having a pre-supper drink. 'It'll be just like your father to try to persuade her to rejoin the practice, sell up here and live with us.' She turned anxious eyes on her daughter, who immediately shook her head.

'She wouldn't entertain the idea, not for one moment, and I'm sure Dad won't ask her.'

She mentioned this to her father, though, when they were shopping in the town next morning. 'Mum seems to think you've got plans for spiriting Prue back into the practice,' she said as they hurried across the traffic-halted road before the green man disappeared.

He laughed at the idea, as she'd known he would. 'Your mother's imagination goes into overdrive sometimes,' he said. 'What I wish Prue would do, though, is get herself a dog. I've got a grand little bitch at the surgery now, who's in need of a home. She's small, spayed, of mixed breed, and about two years old. Her owner got killed on the road last week, and Doris—good name for a dog—was brought into me.'

170

'Did you mention it to Prue?'

'Yes, and she wouldn't consider it. Said she was too old to start looking after a dog again which, seeing how fit she is, I felt was a lame excuse.'

'Still, it's got to be her choice, Dad,' Anna was saying just as he pulled her to a halt and pointed across the road.

'Look over there. . .just passing Boots. . . Isn't that your Mr Easter with a woman in blue? Lost them now, can't see them. . . Ah, there they are, by that poster, by the news-stall. . .just going round the arcade!'

'OK, OK, I can see them—or could—and, yes, it was him!' She had seen him at once, and the usual pinging shock of recognition had hit her full force. He'd been wearing grey and had his jacket off—slung over one shoulder. The girl beside him had been slim and dark; it'd been Julia Trafford. Anna was sure that it was her, for hadn't Alex said she was due back home any day?

'I suppose the girl's his wife?'

Anna shook her head as she and her father walked on. 'He's divorced so, no, but I rather think she's a Doctor Trafford. She's a doctor of research—something to do with equinine diseases.'

'Clever, then? Still, I can't see Easter interested in an air-head. I take it she's his girlfriend?'

'I shouldn't be surprised.'

'You know, it's funny,' Paul Gatton said, steering Anna across the road, 'but I'd have taken him for a married man with a couple of kids.'

Lunch back at The Gables—a cold collation—was a comfortless, dreary affair, with Prue looking pensive and she was most likely, Anna thought, wishing that she wasn't going to Reading; wishing that she was staying at home; perhaps even wishing—for such are the vagaries of human nature—that Great-Nan was still alive and up at the nursing-home, and that she, Prue, was going to visit her to hear all her moans and groans.

She looked happier, though, at three-thirty when she was actually in the car, riding in the front with her son— Diane happy to sit in the back with her feet up and her dark glasses on.

Left to her own devices at last, Anna went into the garden with the idea of weeding and tidying up generally, a task which she very soon found in no way precluded thinking.

And so it was, as she bent and weeded and raked and swept with determined energy, that the glimpse she had had of Simon and Julia making their way past Boots assumed mammoth proportions in her mind, blotting out everything else.

Until she told herself with steadying sternness that Simon's private life was nothing, but nothing, to do with her and that if he was walking past Boots with half the female population of Charding it was still no concern of hers.

A brisk little wind had begun to blow, and she was thinking of going inside when she heard a car stopping at the front gate. Seconds later Alex appeared, making for the front steps and carrying roses somewhat gingerly— perhaps because of possible thorn damage to the front of his shirt. As she called to him he turned and they met halfway across the lawn.

'Pa and I thought Mrs Gatton might like these roses. Hope they're not coals to Newcastle,' he added with a smile.

'They're not. Prue's second crop didn't come to much—' Anna took the flowers '—but the only thing is that she isn't here. She went back to Reading with Mother and Daddy after lunch. She's going to stay with them for a few days.'

'Oh dear,' Alex frowned.

'Unless you want to take them back home, I'd love to have them.' Anna buried her face in the blooms, drawing in the scent of the dark red ones which she loved best.

'Of course. Keep them—I'd like you to have them,' Alex said, agreeing at once when she suggested that he stayed and had some tea.

'I was just thinking of making some.' She was glad he had come, pleased at the thought of some company. Solitude was fine but only, she thought sadly, when one wasn't bedevilled by painful thoughts.

Alex hadn't seen her flat before and he walked around, looking at her pictures and photographs with interest and exclaiming at the fact that she had two sitting-rooms— both of them with views—and admiring her modern kitchen. 'You've made a real home of it, Anna.'

'It *is* my home,' she said.

'Well, yes, of course.' He took the tray from her and she led the way into the sitting-room which overlooked the back garden—overlooked, in fact, several of the neighbouring gardens going up the road. 'Seems to be a lot of activity going on along there,' Alex said, looking away to the right where the top of what looked like a large marquee could be seen.

'It's a wedding. Prue was asked, but of course couldn't go. . .had to cry off at the last minute.' Anna handed him his tea.

'Good day for it.'

'Just about perfect.' She leaned back in her chair, feeling happier by the minute. It was pleasant to sit and talk to Alex about his father and Tom; about yesterday's funeral and the following luncheon party, and about how good it had been to have some time with her father. 'He wants Prue to have a dog,' she said, and he told her that Tom's current craze was to have a pet snake.

'Fortunately Imogen has put her foot down, and with my full backing!'

It was when they were in the kitchen, washing up, that Alex dropped his bombshell. 'You and I could get married,' he said.

Anna caught her breath, swivelling round to face him, unable to believe her ears. Not for one moment had she thought he was joking but, even so, the way he had spoken—so unemotionally—made his words unreal. 'I know we're not romantically in love,' he went on before she could speak, 'but that kind of thing doesn't always last. Affection and friendship do. You're exactly what I want in a wife—I knew that from the first.'

She stared at him as he stood there against the break-fast bar, looking as he always did—smart, and smooth, and brushed. The thought of what marriage to him would bring her reeled through her mind like a film—a lovely home, security, status, children and a good man. For he'd be loyal always, she knew that; he'd never let her down.

But you don't love him, Anna Fellowes, and he doesn't love you. You'd strain at the relationship, certainly strain at making love with him. You can't do it and you know you can't; being 'just friends' isn't enough.

'Alex, I can't! I'm terribly sorry, but I'd have to be in love to marry again, I really would. Being fond of you isn't enough!' All this came out in a tumbled rush, whilst through the open window the sound of wedding party revelry blew in like mocking dust.

'It's all right, don't worry, I expected you to say almost exactly that.' He was grave-faced but didn't, she thought, look particularly upset. He was folding the teatowel he'd been using and hanging it back on the rack. 'You've never been other than honest with me, Anna, so there's nothing to be sorry about. And now, I think, I'd better be going. Tom will be waiting for me. Don't forget to put your roses in water.' He touched them as he passed.

'No, I won't, they're lovely.' She followed him downstairs, and walked with him to the gate.

'See you,' he said, as he got in the car.

'See you,' she said in reply, but these were just words
to cover embarrassment, and their smiles were that kind
too. They would meet again by chance, she knew that,
but never by design, for when marriage has been offered
and the offer turned down, however tactfully, nothing
can be quite the same after that. . .it's a no-go zone.

It was necessary, after Alex had gone, to apply herself
to physical activities again so, between five o'clock and
ten, she cleaned the flat from floor to ceiling, including
its windows—inside and out—at great danger to herself,
the flat being two floors up.

Her reward was sleep—sound sleep—that night, but
on waking in the morning it was to a feeling of bleakness,
even fear, about the future. Why, even the Sunday bells
carolling out from St Peter's Church did nothing to lift
her gloom.

Shortly after nine, when her phone rang, she was still
in the bathroom. Stepping out of the shower, wrapped
around in a towel, she went to answer it. It was probably
Prue ringing up from Reading. All set to be cheery and
bright she lifted the receiver, and almost before she had
sung out, 'Hello' the voice of one of the nursing officers
rattled in her ear.

'Sister, there's been a collision on the motorway. . .
We're on Major Accident Alert. Can you help us out. . .?
Can you report in. . .? We need all the help we can get.
You're at liberty to refuse, of course, but. . .'

'I'll come. . .I'll be there!' Anna's towel slipped
unheeded to her feet.

'Report to Cas. . .thanks. . .goodbye!'

Anna scrambled into her clothes, pinned her name

badge onto her dress and raced down the stairs. She was at the hospital within fifteen minutes, meeting on the way a tide of ambulances and two fire engines speeding to the accident scene.

A team of doctors and nurses, wearing helmets and fluorescent tabards, were piling into a waiting ambulance as she turned into the yard. It was the team, she knew, who would administer to the wounded on site, giving pain-killing injections, setting up IV lines and making decisions as to which of the injured should take the first ambulance.

One of the doctors climbing into the ambulance with a backpack of equipment was Simon. Anna saw him distinctly before the doors were slammed to, and the ambulance, siren wailing, swung out of the yard. He must have been called in before her; he might even, she thought, have been here at the time. Whichever it was, he was on the road now, on the road and geared for action. Perhaps even, like her, feeling apprehensive at what lay ahead.

Inside A and E all areas had been cleared for action. The emergency plan was in operation, and any routine patients who had come in that morning had been evacuated to Outpatients until staff could attend to them.

Equipment was being rushed in, every cubicle stood ready, extra beds and trolleys stood in the bays and doctors and nurses from various wards and sections of the hospital were being co-ordinated by Sister Forrester, who placed Anna on triage with the surgical registrar. This meant that as the casualties arrived she and he would have to sort them into the categories of critical, urgent, non-urgent or dead.

Anna thought about Simon; imagined him in the thick of it on the motorway, working in a mêlée of ambulancemen, fire officers and police; kneeling by the injured staunching wounds, applying temporary splints, setting up drips and drains, comforting the trapped, injecting analgesics and trying to keep up morale.

The waiting was tense and it was almost a relief when the first three ambulances came in, their crews giving vital information as to whether a patient had been unconscious, had been trapped—and for how long—had been having fits, or was showing signs of bleeding internally.

The accident had been a knock-on collision. It appeared that a Jaguar had crashed into the back of a coach, bringing day-trippers into Charding. A second coach, following the Jag, had ploughed into its chassis, a van had hit the second coach and a car had hit the van—the whole lot piling together like a set of children's bricks.

The police arrived; the press arrived; more and more patients arrived. Stretcher after stretcher was wheeled in. It seemed to Anna that she'd been looking down at faces half-obscured by masks, at temporarily splinted limbs, at head collars steadying spines, and hearing moans and cries of pain for hours, and hours, and hours.

Thirty stretcher cases were sorted and passed through for treatment. It was learned that another twenty-five had been sent two miles inland to the county hospital at Bewlis, which was sharing the load.

After the stretcher cases came the walking wounded, many of them elderly, wandering about the department in a state of total shock. One old lady had a broken collar-bone sticking out from her shoulder, and most had torn clothes and bruised faces and limbs.

Many wouldn't rest until they'd heard about their relatives or friends... 'I can't find my Tom; he was sitting beside me and I blacked out, and when I came to he'd gone.' There was a young man with a broken nose begging for news about his wife... 'She's expecting; she's eight months! They made me come on here, but she's still in the wreckage! I want to know the minute she gets here, Nurse!'

Finally, at long last, the medical team came back, including Simon. Anna saw him immediately, pushing through a crowd of reporters into the department, whilst behind him the ambulancemen were pulling a stretcher on which lay a shrouded form. They turned into the first empty cubicle, Simon beckoning to Anna. 'Need your help... Girl died in ambulance...live baby inside her!'

As he ripped off his tabard and helmet Anna fetched a surgical tray, not that he needed many instruments—not with the mother dead, her face covered, only the huge mound of belly exposed. And how different it was from an ordinary Caesar. The essence of this one was speed.

There was little bleeding when the abdomen was incised and none when the uterus was cut. Only the spurt of amniotic fluid, drenching them, was the same. The child was curled there, already moving. Simon felt for and pulled up the legs, holding the tiny body up-ended whilst he disentangled the cord.

It was a girl-child, and lusty. She began yelling at once as he handed her to Anna, covered in vernix and dark hair plastered down.

Anna soothed and wiped her, and rolled her in a towel after Simon had cut the cord. Sister Forrester appeared, alerted by its cries. 'Dear God, what a business!' She went into the cubicle and came out again. 'Have we a name? Do we know who she is...*was*?' she corrected herself, looking grim.

'There's a husband,' Anna told her, 'with facial injuries, awaiting his turn in Minor Ops. I was speaking to him—his name's Robert Massingham. They've got his details at the Desk.'

'Then I'll have to go and see him, and *now*.' Anita Forrester's eyes closed, then opened again as she turned and made her way to the waiting area outside Minor Ops. Simon, with a staff nurse from Paeds, was tidying the dead woman's body. Anna, with the child quiet now in her arms and trying to nuzzle her breast, took the lift to Baby Care, where she handed the infant to Rose.

Returning to Casualty, she found that many of the more seriously wounded had been passed through to ICU, or were being prepared for surgery. The orthopaedic team were working full out in two of the theatres, whilst nursing staff, orderlies and porters rushed extra beds to the wards.

The police were dealing with the flood of relatives who were converging on the hospital and the switchboard was awash with calls, whilst over the road in the disused Physical Medicine building the hospital administrator was giving out carefully edited data to the clamouring press.

Anna learned from Simon that the young mother who had died and her husband, Robert, had been travelling to Charding to visit his parents for the day. 'They were in the first coach, which had the worst casualties. Eight people were killed in there. She was trapped by the neck when it overturned; he was thrown out. He's got a fractured cheek-bone and septum. I've just broken the news to him, and told him about his child.'

'I expect his parents will come.'

'I'm sure they will.' He flung a swab into a bowl. 'I'll use that silk thread, I think. . .yes, that's the one. You all right, Mr Harris?' He took the threaded needle from Anna. They were stitching the head of an old man who'd been all but scalped by jagged metal. He was due for admission to one of the wards once he'd had his anti-tet.

He was astonishingly calm about his injury. 'I live on

my own, you see, so no one to worry about. . . Makes a difference, dear. I come down here every year for a treat. Charding's a grand place.'

He was wheeled away and after that, amongst all grades of staff—for no one worried about status and protocol at such a crisis time—Simon and Anna worked non-stop, cleaning and stitching wounds, setting up drips, giving injections, binding strains and sprains, taking blood for cross-matching and reuniting frightened children with their parents.

Someone put a mug of tea at Anna's elbow, but she never got round to drinking it. There was too much to do; there was no let-up and yet, amazingly, at a little before two p.m. Accident and Emergency, whilst not clear of casualties, was able to cope with its own on-shift staff again and all 'locums' were released.

'You and I,' Simon said, catching up with Anna when she came out of the washroom, 'are going over to the Taverner for a brandy, and then I'll walk you home.'

'But our cars. . .' she protested, not very forcibly.

'We'll leave them where they are. I don't have to tell you that we can't drink and drive.'

'I don't like brandy.' She knew she was weakening and she needed company. After the last five shocking hours, to go home alone. . .and there was no one *at* home. . .just wasn't bearable.

'Look upon it as medicinal.' He was steering her out into the yard, where the brightness of the sun made them squint and where the soft, warm breeze blowing in from the sea had a poignant quality, bringing ready tears to her eyes. 'You see what I mean?' He bent over her slightly. 'You need. . .we *both* need a stiffener, so over the road we go.'

She hadn't even thought about how he was feeling, she realised a few minutes later as she sipped her brandy and felt it hit her throat in a series of bombs. It must have been terrible on that motorway and he'd been one of the first on the scene.

He was a surgeon and well used to blood and guts, but not spilled all over the road. He wasn't used to seeing people trapped in wreckage, nor laying them out on the verge. It was small wonder he looked so gaunt and strained—the little scar to the right of his chin was showing up plainly, as it did when he was disturbed.

They talked about the accident, for to ignore it was impossible. The morning's events were too close for that—they couldn't be pushed away as though they hadn't happened. 'We did a good job,' Simon said presently, staring down into his glass.

'It was incredible how everyone pulled together.' Anna was beginning to feel the effect of the brandy and felt as if she was floating above the bar stool.

'You were rung up at the flat, were you?' she heard Simon ask.

'Yes, I'd only just got out of bed. How about you?'

'Me. . .? Oh, I was practically hauled in off the street. I was on my way to see Bill in Residents when one of the paramedics hailed me, told me what had happened and I found myself volunteering to go out with the medical team.'

'I saw you getting into the ambulance as I turned into the yard.' Anna was still fighting that floating sensation, trying to ward it off.

'I spotted you—' Simon smiled at her, and she saw his face through a haze '—when I came in with that poor dead girl. I couldn't believe my luck when I saw you standing there. . .'

'I was on triage,' she said. 'I'd only just come off it. I wasn't just standing about.' Drink could make one assertive, and she caught his look of surprise.

'Well, whatever it was I was lucky to have you helping me.'

'I didn't do much.' She wasn't convinced.

'You did a very great deal.' He shifted slightly and the side of his hand touched hers on the counter, whilst over its top and behind the barman and behind the row of small bottles at the back, they could see themselves in the mirror running the length of the bar.

We look like a couple, Anna thought, liking what she saw and wanting to keep on looking, but the floating sensation was affecting her vision and everything seemed to blur.

'Anna!' She was aware of Simon swivelling his stool to face her. 'Anna, are you feeling all right?'

'Not really.' She started to giggle, then determinedly made herself stop. 'I'm hung-over, Simon. It's my empty stomach. I've not eaten since seven last night.'

'Great Scott! Why didn't I *think*?' He thumped the counter-top. 'I'm afraid they'll have stopped serving lunches now, but we could have a bar snack—a sandwich or a burger—'

'No, thanks, I've had enough of today and I'd rather get home,' she told him bluntly, for it was necessary—in fact, vital—to get away from him fast before she went the whole hog and told him that she loved him. . .yes, loved him, *loved* him. . .and had done so from the day he'd told her that he would trust her with his life. He wouldn't want that—declarations like that would send him running for cover, and fill *her* with embarrassment and mortification when she had to meet him again.

Once out in the street he held her securely by the elbow, just in case, Anna thought wryly, I fall flat on my face—not that there was any danger of that now, for she seemed to have sobered up. The air hadn't made her feel worse but better, and she gratefully drew it in. It was a good idea to *walk* home too; it was good to stride out.

'I expect you want to get home to see as much of your parents as possible while they are here,' Simon remarked as they waited at the pedestrian crossing near the Palace Pier.

'Oh, they're not there. They went back yesterday, taking Prue with them.' Someone trod on the back of Anna's heel and she gave a little yelp.

Simon tightened his grasp on her, saying, way above her head, 'I'm sure it'll help Mrs Gatton to be away for a day or two.'

'Yes, that's what my father thought.'

'I was glad to be able to meet him.' They were crossing the road in a rush, meeting the crowd from the other side.

'Dad's a love; we've always been close,' Anna shouted above the din of a coach unloading its passengers at the kerb. It was then without warning, like a stab in the chest, that her thoughts swung back to this morning's crash when two coaches had been involved; when their passengers, instead of piling out on the sea-front—laughing and ready for fun—had come to Charding by ambulance, and some hadn't reached it at all.

Simon was thinking the same way she was. She could tell that by the way he halted and tensed for a second, then continued to march her on even more quickly, so much so that she felt as if she'd got flying feet. 'Simon, hold on, you've missed the turning,' she managed to say at last.

'Not missed it, passed it,' he informed her tersely, 'which isn't quite the same thing. I'm taking you home to share the lunch Mrs Gill will have left for me. It'll be cold but I can heat up some soup, and before you say no I need company, and I think you do—just for an hour or two.'

'I'd like that,' she said, and caught the faint look of

astonishment on his face before he hurried her on past the Lawns Hotel, and into Andover Square.

It was the third time she had been to his house, and as they turned up the drive Buzz was there to greet Simon with glee and to regard her with his usual look of suspicion and warning. . .touch me if you dare.

They ate cold meats and salad in the little orchard, with a cloth spread on the grass. The patio, in full sun, wasn't restful that afternoon, but under the trees, which filtered the sunlight, all was shaded and cool—a far better option than eating in the house on such a brilliant day.

Perhaps because of the picnic atmosphere and the casual way they ate, with plates on their laps like the day-trippers down on the beach, there was no tension between them—just contentment and easiness—and Anna rejoiced. We have it in us to heal one another, she thought, and marvelled anew. I can make his fears recede and die, as he can mine.

After they'd eaten he went into the house to make coffee, and it was when he returned—dipping his head under the low-hanging trees—that she sensed a change in him, and in herself. Tiny little spears of panicky excitement were flickering between them, and neither met the other's eyes. Anna found herself holding her breath.

She saw one of the empty cups roll on its side as he set the tray on the ground. He was half turned from her, white shirt strained across his back, but now he was turning and kneeling beside her. 'Anna, darling girl!' He pressed her back, his breath on her face as he unzipped the front of her dress, and, as she cried his name and lifted her arms to pull him on top of her, she saw his need of her dark in his eyes a second before they rolled together. . .grappled together. . .and made love in the grass.

He held her close for a long time afterwards, bringing her back to earth. Then, sitting up, they laughed in wonder, and perhaps in relief. They even drank the neglected coffee, and it tasted ambrosial. 'I'm surprised it's still here!' She had never felt so thirsty in her life.

'*We're* still here,' he teased.

'I'm surprised about that as well!'

'I love you, Anna...you know that, don't you?'

To hear him say that was bliss. 'I love you too.' She put her head on his shoulder. 'I love you too,' she repeated because it was so good to be able to admit it... It meant so much not to have to turn away, and lie about hating him. This is an affair, she told herself, and we're right at the start of it, and one day he'll end it but I'm glad it's happening; I'll take each day as it comes.

'Will you marry me?' He loosened his hold a little and looked down into her face. 'Darling girl, will you marry me?' he repeated when, at first, she said nothing at all.

'But it's not what you want... You've always said...' Her mouth was agape. He put his finger between her teeth and smiled. 'Seems to me,' he sighed, 'that I said too many things, trying to save my face.

'It wasn't I who felt shackled in marriage, but Caroline. She quickly got bored with being the wife of a junior doctor. I was twenty-four when we got married, and had to work all hours. She was chafing at the bit after the first year, and I quickly realised that I should never have asked her to marry me. I felt it was all my fault.

'She was an artist, freelance; designed jackets for books; when she was offered employment by a New York publishing house, off she went. Love died like a withering bush, and I vowed, never again.

'You, on the other hand,' he went on before she could

speak, 'had a happy marriage, so felt confident enough
to want to put to sea again.'

'I loved my husband, yes,' she said, 'I never ever
stopped. I even loved him after death, if you can possibly
understand that. I wasn't happy, though; it wasn't like
that. It wasn't a happy marriage. Danny hadn't got it in
him to be faithful—his affairs were legion but I just kept
on, hoping that he'd change.'

'Great Scott, I had no idea!' It was his turn to stare.

'Well, I didn't give you any clues, did I, nor anyone
else? My parents knew, and so did Prue, but they were
the only ones. I thought,' she went on, recognising that
this was plain-speaking time, 'that you might be the same
sort of man, partly because I was attracted to you
so easily—practically at first sight—and because you
were so. . .personable. I thought those were the danger
signs.'

'So you went around with Marriner.'

'Only as a friend. He knew I couldn't be anything
more—I told him that from the first. Anyway—' her
chin lifted '—as we seem to be clearing the decks, what
about the trendy Doctor Julia Trafford?'

'She was an amusing companion for an occasional
outing; we were never, ever lovers. There hasn't been
anyone important in my life for a long time now. Having
confessed. . .' he smiled, but looked anxious as he turned
her face to his '. . .will you take a chance with me, Anna?
Will you let me look after you, cherish and adore you
from this day forward? Will you be my wife?'

'Of course I will.' Her fingers smoothed the frown
from his brow. 'Of course I will,' she told him simply.
'You're my dearest, dearest love.'

Then, getting to their feet and linking arms, they went
into the house.

*   *   *

They were married by special licence ten days later, making the Andover Square house their home, and as time went on Prue let the top flat to another artist who liked the north-facing room.

Anna continued with her job, but left it when she became pregnant with their first child. Andrew Simon Easter was born with the minimum of fuss the following summer, and all was happiness. Anna had another child—a little girl—two years later, and in that same year Alex Marriner and Imogen Rayland married in West Beldon Parish Church, causing one or two eyebrows to rise—particularly Amy Benson's, who had always nurtured the hope that one day Imogen would make her home with her.

Anna was delighted for them both. . . 'But I suppose you're going to say,' she teased Simon when they heard of the engagement, 'I suppose you're going to say that she's far too old for him. . .obsessed as you are with age!'

'It's you I'm obsessed with, and always will be—and what's more, you know it,' he muttered thickly into her hair as he turned out the bedside light.

MILLS & BOON®

Medical Romance™

COMING NEXT MONTH

A MIDWIFE'S CHALLENGE by Frances Crowne

Katy Woods resolved never to get involved with men after her disastrous marriage to a bigamist—until she met Dr Mark Hammond. He was irresistible—until she discovered the truth about his ex-girlfriend, which was a haunting reminder of her past...

FULL RECOVERY by Lilian Darcy

Camberton Hospital

Helen Darnell suspected her husband of twenty years, Nick, to be having an affair with a beautiful doctor. Helen tried to quell her fears believing that Nick was faithful to her. Their marriage was teetering on the edge of destruction and only one thing could save it—the truth.

DOCTOR ACROSS THE LAGOON by Margaret Holt

Lucinda Hallcross-Spriggs' journey to Italy for a medical conference took an unexpected turn when she met the devilishly handsome Dr Pino Ponti. She soon succumbed to his relentless charm, but with his restless heart and uneasy past, she surely had no part to play in his future.

LAKELAND NURSE by Gill Sanderson

Zanne Ripley's application for Medical School was unsuccessful—and all because of Dr Neil Calder. Now she had to work with him at the Mountain Activities Centre, but his charm soon broke down her defences. But Neil had a secret...

Available from WH Smith, John Menzies, Volume One, Forbuoys, Martins, Woolworths, Tesco, Asda, Safeway and other paperback stockists.

MILLS & BOON®

Back by Popular Demand

BETTY NEELS

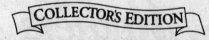

COLLECTOR'S EDITION

**A collector's edition of favourite titles
from one of the world's best-loved
romance authors.**

Mills & Boon are proud to bring back these
sought after titles, now reissued in beautifully
matching volumes and presented as one
cherished collection.

Don't miss these unforgettable titles, coming
next month:

Title #21 ALL ELSE CONFUSION
Title #22 NEVER SAY GOODBYE

Available wherever
Mills & Boon books are sold

*Available from WH Smith, John Menzies, Forbuoys, Martins, Tesco,
Asda, Safeway and other paperback stockists.*

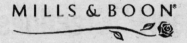

MILLS & BOON®

Four remarkable family reunions,
Four fabulous new romances—

Don't miss our exciting Mother's Day Gift Pack
celebrating the joys of motherhood with love, laughter
and lots of surprises.

SECOND-TIME BRIDE   Lynne Graham
INSTANT FATHER   Lucy Gordon
A NATURAL MOTHER   Cathy Williams
YESTERDAY'S BRIDE   Alison Kelly

Special Promotional Price of £6.30—
4 books for the price of 3

Available: February 1997

'Happy' Greetings!

Would you like to win a year's supply of Mills & Boon® books?
Well you can and they're free! Simply complete the
competition below and send it to us by 31st August 1997. The
first five correct entries picked after the closing date will each
win a year's subscription to the Mills & Boon series of their
choice. What could be easier?

ACSPPMTHYHARSI

_ _ _ _ _ _   _ _ _ _ _ _ _

TPHEEYPSARA

_ _ _ _ _   _ _ _ _ _

RAHIHPYBDYTAP

_ _ _ _ _ _   _ _ _ _ _ _ _

NHMYRTSPAAPNERUY

_ _ _ _ _   _ _ _ _ _ _   _ _ _ _ _ _ _

DYVLTEPYAANINSEPAH

_ _ _ _ _ _   _ _ _ _ _ _ _ _   _ _ _

YAYPNAHPEREW

_ _ _ _ _ _   _ _ _ _   _ _ _

DMHPYAHRYOSETPA

_ _ _ _ _ _   _ _ _ _ _ _   _ _ _ _

VRHYPNARSAEYNPIA

_ _ _ _ _   _ _ _ _ _ _ _ _ _ _

Please turn over for details of how to enter ☞

How to enter...

There are eight jumbled up greetings overleaf, most of which you will probably hear at some point throughout the year. Each of the greetings is a 'happy' one, i.e. the word 'happy' is somewhere within it. All you have to do is identify each greeting and write your answers in the spaces provided. Good luck!

When you have unravelled each greeting don't forget to fill in your name and address in the space provided and tick the Mills & Boon® series you would like to receive if you are a winner. Then simply pop this page into an envelope (you don't even need a stamp) and post it today. Hurry—competition ends 31st August 1997.

Mills & Boon 'Happy' Greetings Competition
FREEPOST, Croydon, Surrey, CR9 3WZ

Please tick the series you would like to receive if you are a winner

Presents™ ❏   Enchanted™ ❏   Medical Romance™ ❏
Historical Romance™ ❏   Temptation® ❏

Are you a Reader Service Subscriber?   Yes ❏   No ❏

Ms/Mrs/Miss/Mr _____

(BLOCK CAPS PLEASE)

Address _____

_____

_____ Postcode _____

(I am over 18 years of age)

One application per household. Competition open to residents of the UK and Ireland only.
You may be mailed with other offers from other reputable companies as a result of this application. If you would prefer not to receive such offers, please tick box. ❏

mps MAILING PREFERENCE SERVICE

C7B